COZY MYSTERIES FOR SPRING

# DAISY LANDISH

Editing by Jessica McKenna
Cover by Daisy Landish

BEACHES AND TRAILS
PUBLISHING

# ABOUT THE AUTHOR

Daisy Landish is a romance and cozy mystery author living in the UK, whose clean and sweet stories have tugged at readers' heartstrings across the pond and beyond. When she's not writing, Daisy spends her time reading, hiking at dawn, and riding into the sunset on her horse, Rosebud.

Join Daisy's Newsletter for updates and giveaways!
www.daisylandishromance.com

- facebook.com/daisylandishromance
- x.com/daisy_landish
- instagram.com/beachesandtrailspublishing
- amazon.com/author/daisylandish
- bookbub.com/authors/daisy-landish
- goodreads.com/Daisy_Landish

# ALSO BY DAISY LANDISH

# THE FELINE CAPER

## A PINE GROVE MYSTERY

# PROLOGUE
## TIMMS RESIDENCE

A chill wind pierced through Verna Timms, making her arthritic joints ache. Shadows built along the streets surrounding her backyard, sending a shiver down her spine. Pine Grove, New England, had once seemed the perfect place to retire. Verna felt good about residing close to her remaining family in a place she knew well.

"Persephone?" she called, rattling the bag of treats. Fall was near its end, and the nights were bitterly cold. "Persephone, where are you, baby?"

She strained her ears for a distant mewling, but there were no answering sounds. The rest of the cats twined around her feet, crying for their supper. It had taken her hours to round them all up. There was still no sight of the elegant Persephone.

Somewhere in the growing darkness, a dog barked. The yipping of coyotes answered. Verna shook the treat bag harder, hoping desperately that her cat would return. It wasn't safe out here. Verna was worried that something terrible had happened. Her heart ached whenever she thought of everything that could go wrong.

*This can't be happening,* she thought.

Some of her neighbors sneered at her, calling her everything from 'crazy cat lady' to 'hoarder.' But she wasn't—yes, she had a lot of cats in her care. She had fostered a poor kitty many times until it could move on to its forever home. She only kept the ones nobody else wanted.

Ever since her dear husband had passed on, Verna had been rescuing cats nobody else would take. Blind, missing limbs, or angry, spitting cats. Every one she brought into her home got warmth, love, and food.

She meticulously cleaned out the various litter boxes in the house every day and spent hours sweeping, vacuuming, and cleaning. She even had her nephew come around to help her build a safe enclosure in the backyard so her kitties could enjoy the outdoors without being in danger from passing cars or predators.

The little black cat named Hades placed his paws on her knee, letting out an extra plaintive yowl. Helplessness swept through Verna.

"Persephone," she called one last time.

Nothing. Darkness was growing even thicker around her, and she reluctantly turned back to her house. She was angry but also worried. This couldn't have been an accident. But she couldn't bear to think about anyone deliberately hurting her kitties.

Verna opened the door, letting the cats stream back into its warmth. Only Hades stayed out. He stared with pricked-up ears, and his tail flicked back and forth to the property line.

Verna hobbled toward the fence. "Persephone?"

Hades' fur stood on end, and he hissed. The wind picked up, bringing more cries from coyotes with it. At the edge of town, backed onto a land conservation as she was, Verna was reminded that the wildlife was never very far away. Tears pricked her eyes as she shook the bag in one last desperate attempt to entice Persephone back.

Nothing.

She turned and swooped Hades into her arms. Cuddling him to her chest, she hurried inside and shut the door. As the warmth of her home thawed her bones, Verna prayed that, wherever she was, Persephone would survive the night.

# CHAPTER 1

## MAIN STREET, PINE GROVE

Peter lifted his face to the glowing sun, reveling in the strange burst of summer-like conditions the day offered. Despite the frosty nights, the daytime was pleasant. Add in the colorful hues of the New England fall hanging on, his usual morning jog had been exceptionally enjoyable, even this close to winter.

"Woof!" While trotting at this side, Sam wagged his tail as he attempted to catch a falling leaf.

Peter smiled at his dog. It wasn't just the weather that put him in such a good mood. The kind vet, Dr. Jessica Stern, who helped him out with Sam, was meeting them for lunch at the café on main street. With such a beautiful day, they had already taken advantage of the open patio.

As Peter approached, however, he was surprised to see Jessica wasn't alone. An older woman with greying hair sat at the table beside her. The woman's hands were cupped around a black mug, while Jessica had a mug herself that was pushed to one side. She patted the woman's arm, her brows pinched together.

Jessica was always ready to greet Peter with a smile. Seeing her like this upset him. Questions raced through his mind. What was going on?

He stepped up to the table and cleared his throat. Both Jessica and the older woman jumped. Looking closer, he saw this woman wearing a midnight blue floor-length dress. A shawl was wrapped around her shoulders, and her short grey hair was styled impeccably. She was clearly a woman who took pride in her appearance, even if her fashion sense was somewhat dated.

"Peter, I'm glad you're here." Jessica smiled at him, but it seemed strained.

"Woof!" Sam wagged his tail as he trotted under the table to put his head in the older woman's lap. His nose twitched, and he licked her hand.

The old woman gave the dog a watery smile. "You're a real sweetheart, aren't you?"

Peter took his seat and tied Sam's leash to the chair.

"Verna, this is my friend Peter," Jessica said, nodding toward him. "He's brilliant at solving knotty problems. I'm sure he can help with this."

Verna turned toward him and squinted. "Ah, yes. The Myers boy. Everyone's talking about how you solved poor Mr. Dalton's murder when that incompetent Captain Donnelly was too busy being a... well, some things a lady should not say, even when they're true."

Peter had to bite back a laugh. With the way Sam responded to her and her way of talking, he was quickly finding he liked Verna. "What seems to be the problem at hand?"

Verna took a deep, shuddering breath, but it appeared she couldn't speak. She turned to Jessica.

With a sigh, Jessica explained. "Verna runs a cat sanctuary and fosters strays out of her home. She takes in any abandoned cats she can from the shelter. She works to get them back into peak health, and if she can find new homes for them, she does so. If they cannot be adopted for whatever reason, she keeps them until they pass on."

"That sounds admirable," Peter drawled. He was confused about what the problem was. "Is there a problem with your cats?"

"Three have gone missing in the last three weeks," Verna said. Her voice shook like she was on the verge of tears. Sam whined, and she rubbed his ears fondly.

Sam must not be bothered by cats, Peter thought. Verna must smell like them.

"I'm sorry that they're missing, but cats go missing all the time," Peter said.

Verna shook her head firmly. "I take good care of my cats. I don't allow them to go wandering around the neighborhood. They'd get eaten by coyotes or hit by cars. Not to mention the number of cruel people who would torment and kill them for no reason."

Peter frowned. "Then how are they going missing?"

"That's what we're worried about," Jessica sighed.

"The police are ignoring me entirely. My cats all got out yesterday, and I do not know how. I keep the doors and windows shut. I have an enclosure in my backyard for them, and the police keep saying that I must have left the door open, but I know I didn't."

Peter folded his hands on the table. He wasn't sure exactly what Jessica thought he could do about this. Even if Verna insisted that she couldn't have accidentally let her cats out, there could be many things that she could have overlooked, especially if it had happened three times already.

Before Peter could say anything, though, the server came over. He was chewing a piece of gum, smacking his lips obnoxiously as he asked, "Do you want anything?"

Peter frowned. He'd never been treated so rudely here before. "I'll get a cup of coffee."

"Fine. But you better all clear out soon. I hate cats." The server eyed Verna with disgust.

Sam growled.

"Hush, Sam," Peter said, and Sam fell silent. He faced the server. "A cup of coffee, and if we are being kicked out, please let your manager do it rather than taking it on yourself. Besides, I don't see any cats here. Do you?"

The server wrinkled his nose and stomped over to a table at the other end of the patio. The woman who sat there was glaring at him, Verna, and Jessica. Another cat-hater, perhaps? It was ridiculous. Yes, it appeared Verna was in some ways the typical 'cat lady,' but she was well-groomed and articulate, and there wasn't a trace of cat hair on her.

Something in his gut told Peter there was more to this story after all. He was ashamed of himself for jumping to conclusions already. Between the apparent hostility from the server and the woman in the corner, he was getting the feeling that something was up.

"Can you tell me about the cats?" Peter asked.

Verna shifted in her seat, her eyes growing misty. "First, it was Ares. He was always a fighter, a scrappy little guy who had had it rough in life. He was feral growing up and was never fully comfortable inside. I can understand him finding some escape route and taking off. That was three weeks ago."

Peter nodded.

"Then, last week, Hera disappeared. She was always curious and loved to spend time in the 'catio,' the enclosure in my backyard," Verna explained. "She took every opportunity she could to get out my front door and play in the yard, but she never went past the fence and always came for treats."

Jessica gave Peter a significant look as though they were just getting to the part where the tale got suspicious.

"And the third one?" Peter pressed.

"Yesterday, when I came home from volunteering at the library, I saw that the catio was open. All the cats were gone. I searched for hours and got back all twelve, except Persephone."

Peter's eyes widened. "Twelve? You have twelve cats?"

"For the time being," Verna said.

Jessica reached to pat her shoulder comfortingly. "We've had a lot of abandoned animals come into the clinic lately. People treat cats like throwaway pets and just dump them on the side of the road."

Peter still thought that was an awful lot. "But is it even legal to have that many cats?"

"I have special permission from the city," Verna said, sounding put out. "I am a sanctuary and foster, after all."

"Right." Peter nodded, feeling a little chagrinned. Even so, twelve cats? How did she take care of them all?

Verna's lip trembled, but she straightened her shoulders and continued. "Persephone is a beautiful old Persian cat. She's twenty years old."

"Persians normally live twelve to seventeen years," Jessica murmured.

An ancient cat, then. She must be well taken care of.

Verna stroked her thumb across Sam's head. "Persephone hated going outside. She even refused the catio. She liked sitting on her pillow in the front window and watching the birds or napping in the sunshine."

"Can we count on you to look for her?" Jessica asked, her eyes never leaving Peter's face.

"I can't promise I'll find anything out. But I'll do my best," Peter promised. "Something about this just doesn't add up."

# CHAPTER 2

## POLICE STATION

Captain Donnelly looked like he was ready to kick Peter out before Peter even said a word. As Peter entered, he sat behind his desk with an annoyed look on his face. Though his hands were folded over a file folder, Peter caught the reflection of a TV show from the captain's computer screen on the framed photograph behind him.

"What do you want, Myers?" Donnelly snapped.

Peter sat in the chair across from Donnelly. He wasn't about to let the man intimidate him. From the years he worked with the FBI as a lawyer, Peter had seen that tactic used far too often. The best way to deal with a blustering type of police officer like this was to remain calm and in control.

"I'm here to ask you if you've looked into the reports of missing animals from Verna Timms," Peter said.

Donnelly stared at him before he burst into laughter.

Peter frowned. "What exactly is so funny?"

"That crazy old cat lady has you running as her errand boy, has she?" Donnelly asked. He slapped his knee, still laughing. "No, I haven't looked into any missing cat reports. Who cares? They're just cats."

Peter felt himself bristling and fought his anger down. He had always preferred dogs over cats, but he understood why people like Verna would love them. Right now, he was strongly reminded of Jessica telling him cats were 'throw away' animals. No creature deserved to be treated that way.

Peter knew he would not get anywhere appealing to Donnelly's humanity. So, he went for a different approach. "Aren't you at all concerned that the missing animals might indicate that someone is breaking into Mrs. Timms' house?"

"You might be from here, but you've been gone too long, Myers." Donnelly clasped his hands over his belly, smiling as he leaned back in his chair.

He was baiting Peter, trying to get under his skin. But Peter would not let him have the pleasure. He arched an eyebrow at the captain. "And what do you mean by that?"

"What I mean is that Old Timms is a crazy cat lady. I'm not wasting my time or police resources trying to find her missing cats just because she's so old and crazy that she can't remember to shut the door."

Peter reflected on the fact that every time he came to this station, his opinion of Donnelly and the police working here grew even lower. "You really think it's something like that? She seems to be mentally sound to me."

Donnelly rolled his eyes. "If you have too much time on your hands, why don't you take that mutt of yours and go hunting for the cats yourself?"

"Have you even looked at her house? Done any sort of investigation?"

"You're wasting my time." Donnelly grabbed a pencil and started scribbling on the papers before him.

It was clear Peter would not get anything from him. Donnelly was already watching his TV show when Peter shut the door to his office.

Peter headed outside, frustrated and angry from being dismissed. The way Donnelly talked about Verna and her cats was so callous! It was terrible. Clearly, Jessica and Peter were the only ones who cared about the situation.

Once in his car and heading home, Peter decided he would have to do some research on cats. Mainly, he needed to know just how far a cat would roam. And why would an elderly cat who preferred her days napping in the sunshine, not wanting to step outside, suddenly disappear into the unknown world?

# CHAPTER 3

## MYERS RESIDENCE

Sam lay on his bed in the kitchen, stretched out with his paws pointed in the air. Though he appeared to be sleeping, Peter occasionally caught his eyes winking open in the stove's general direction. Peter had to laugh.

"I think Sam knows we're cooking a steak for him," he said to Jessica.

Jessica was at the long counter, making her famous bacon guacamole. Even though Sam was getting a steak today, the humans had decided on taco night. Peter thought about how Sam had gotten very used to having food for himself when Peter had his supper.

"You don't think I'm developing bad habits in him, do you?" Peter asked worriedly.

Jessica laughed. "Look at him, lying there all calm and serene. Bad habits would be if he were getting underfoot or begging. He's a good boy. Aren't you Sam?"

Sam lifted his head and wagged his tail. "Woof," he said in agreement.

Jessica tossed him a small piece of bacon. Sam sniffed it and looked at Peter.

"Oh, look. He's asking for permission," Jessica said.

"Go ahead," Peter said.

Sam wagged his tail again and licked the bacon off the floor. Peter smiled proudly at him. Sam was a wonderful dog. Peter wouldn't have ever thought he would have such a delightful companion when he first saw the thin, abused dog in the forest. But Sam had proven himself many times over.

"Have you made any discoveries in Verna's case?" Jessica asked as she put the rest of the bacon into the guacamole.

Peter winced. He had been dreading this conversation ever since he had finished his research. "I'm not sure. I researched cats and talked to a couple of Verna's neighbors."

Jessica set the bowl aside and leaned against the counter, staring at him.

Peter flipped Sam's steak. It was almost done. "If I'm honest... I'm not sure there is a case here at all."

"Why not?" Jessica's tone was strained.

"Well..." Peter was hesitant to explain his findings. Though he was pretty certain there wasn't more to this situation than he had already found, he also didn't want to disappoint Jessica. He liked her and hated to let her down.

Jessica turned fully to him and folded her arms. "Well, what? You can tell me, Peter. I'm a big girl."

"The truth is, I don't think there is much of a case at all," Peter admitted.

Disappointment filled Jessica's eyes.

"I'm sorry," Peter said, hating to have to say all this. "It's not that I don't believe something is happening. I just don't think there is anything nefarious."

"All right. What do you think is happening, then?" Jessica's voice was still strained.

Peter took the steak off the stove to let it cool before feeding it to Sam. As it rested on the plate, he carried their taco toppings to the kitchen table. He wasn't sure how he was going to tell Jessica his suspicions.

"First, let's talk about Ares and Hera, the first two cats that went missing. Verna said that Ares was an outdoor cat that hated to be inside. It makes sense that he'd take off if he had the chance."

Jessica helped carry the fixings over to the kitchen. "Yes, but Verna is always careful. She never let them out except in the enclosed catio."

"There are many ways a determined cat could find a way out of the house," Peter pointed out. He went back to the steak and cut it into strips for Sam. "Verna has twelve cats. It can't be easy to keep track of all of them."

Jessica shook her head. "She takes too good care of them for Ares to have just gotten out because she wasn't paying attention."

"I didn't say that," Peter insisted. "I only meant that if he didn't want to be there, he could have left without her noticing. Cats can be sneaky."

Jessica opened the fridge and pulled out a pitcher of water. "And Hera?"

"Verna said she liked to find ways out of the house and hang out in the backyard, correct?"

"Yes."

Peter nodded. "Then she probably got out—perhaps the same way Ares did—and either roamed or was taken by an animal from the yard, or even some misguided human who thought she was being abused took her home with them."

"I… suppose," Jessica said doubtfully.

"From my research, cats can roam up to two and a half miles from home and will go hide somewhere to die." Peter hated bringing this up. Verna clearly loved her cats. "You said Persephone had outlived her normal lifespan already."

Jessica shook her head emphatically. "No. She hated being outside and wouldn't have left 'to go die.' She would have wanted to be comfortable. I'm her vet, and she was in perfect health. Much better condition than many cats younger than her."

"Jessica—"

"You talked to Verna's neighbors but didn't go to see her house yourself?" Jessica put her hands on her hips, her eyes crackling with irritation.

"I—" Peter cut himself off, chagrinned. He had no excuse.

"If you just went to her house and saw everything there, you would know. Verna is a sweet lady, and despite what you saw at the café, people like her."

"I guess I'm acting a bit like Donnelly, aren't I?" Peter admitted. "I'm sorry."

The tension in Jessica's shoulders melted away. "So, you'll look into it more?"

"Yes."

Jessica smiled at him. "Thank you."

"Sure thing," Peter said. He still wasn't convinced anything was happening, but Jessica was right. He couldn't just dismiss Verna so easily.

He pulled a chair for Jessica and put Sam's steak on the floor.

"I'll go see her tomorrow," he promised.

# CHAPTER 4
## TIMMS RESIDENCE

Peter let out a heavy breath as he pulled to a stop in the quiet cul-de-sac Verna Timms lived on. He took a moment to gaze around the neighborhood, getting his bearings. It was clear these buildings were older but were all well-cared for. The yards were neatly trimmed, and the trees had all lost their leaves to prepare for winter. Most yards were empty, but a few already had blow-up Christmas decorations.

Verna's house was at the end of the cul-de-sac. From Peter's research, he knew her property was against a land conservatory. That explained the wide field behind the house, edged by a forest a quarter-mile away. Coyotes were a common site in this area. Not a safe place for cats.

Peter shook his head as he stepped out of his car. He hadn't told Jessica, but he had heard from one of Verna's neighbors that they had seen Verna leaving the doors to her house open more and more lately.

Unfortunately, no matter how much Verna loved her cats, her mental facilities could suffer here as she grew older. Peter was uncomfortable knowing he might be investigating a case of early-onset dementia or Alzheimer's.

He wasn't sure what would be worse, one of those diseases or if someone really was stealing her cats.

The front porch was screened in, and as he approached, Peter saw a pitch-black cat on its bed, cleaning its fur. Another cat, a grey-and-white shorthair, sat in the window, watching him with a grumpy expression.

Twelve cats.

Peter grimaced as he opened the screen door. There was a lock on it, but it appeared to be broken. The black cat bolted for the house as soon as he opened the door, disappearing through a square cat flap.

Closing the screen door behind him, Peter moved across the porch to ring the doorbell. He braced himself, preparing for what he was sure he was going to find.

Verna answered a minute later. "Hello, Peter. I'm glad you could come. Come in."

"Thank you," Peter smiled at her as he stepped inside.

To his surprise, the house was spotless. There was no sign of cat hair anywhere, and it had no cat smell at all. The house didn't have that musty sort of scent that came with a lot of elderly people's belongings, either. It seemed Verna took excellent care of her house.

The black cat jumped onto a hall table, batted at Peter's hand, and then jumped off and ran to Verna's feet.

"You'll have to excuse Hades," Verna said as she picked up the black cat and put him on her shoulder. "He comes from a situation where he was terribly abused by a man. It's given him trust issues."

"Understandable," Peter said, thinking about Sam. Anger ran through him. He couldn't understand why anyone would abuse an animal. "Do you have a cleaner?"

Verna led him through the living room. Cats were everywhere, on the windowsill, chairs, and tables. She even had shelves that ran along the ceiling where cats played. They all seemed so pampered and happy.

"Two cleaners," Verna said. "I have them come in on alternating days to help me around the house in case I need to have them come in and take care of my cats."

"Could they forget to close the doors?"

Verna shook her head. "No. I trust them implicitly."

"And you never find that you've forgotten to close or lock the doors?"

"Never."

"What about your porch screen door? I noticed the lock was broken," Peter said cautiously.

Verna's shoulders slumped. "Again? My goodness! I don't understand; I just replaced it the other day."

Peter filed that away in his mind as Verna continued to show him around the house. From what he saw, it was doubtful that the cats had just wandered out. As he talked with Verna, he continued to be impressed with her. He had to admit his concerns that her mental facilities might fail seemed far off.

"What did you do for work before you retired?" Peter asked politely, checking one window. It was locked tight.

"I did government work in D.C. I believe you did as well?" Verna asked. Hades had left, and a sphinx wearing a knitted sweater was now in her arms.

Peter looked at her in a new light. "Government work?"

Verna smirked. "Yes. What did you expect?"

"Not that." Peter thought about it for a moment and smiled at her. "I owe you an apology. I came in with preconceived notions, and I'm ashamed of my behavior."

"I'm used to it, Peter. It's a rare man who can admit when he's wrong."

Peter nodded at her, grateful she was so gracious. "Do you think that your disappearing cats could be connected to your old work? Someone is sending you a message?" he asked.

Verna's gaze darkened. "I have considered that. I hope it's not the case."

"What did you do?"

"Oh… just worked," Verna said, suspiciously vague. She waved a hand. "Let's go out. Come around back; you can check the catio."

The cats followed them as Verna pulled on her coat. She opened the back door, and the cats swarmed around her feet, meowing. She grabbed a bag of treats and tossed them around the impressive enclosure. The cats dashed this way and that having a great time chasing the treats.

"The cat flap to the screen door," Peter started. "Could the cats be escaping through that?"

"I lock it up at night to make sure they can't," Verna replied.

It wasn't big enough for a person to sneak through anyway. Peter examined the catio, but the screens were firmly secured to the frame. Several heated houses sat here and there, allowing the cats to stay warm at night.

"There has been no damage to the catio?" he pressed.

"No. I don't let them come out here at night anymore, either, not since Ares disappeared. I was worried about coyotes breaking in somehow."

Peter hummed, thinking this through. "Would Persephone have left the house if lured by a stranger? For meat, perhaps?"

Verna shook her head. "Never. She loved to sit in her window but cared little about anything else. If someone tried to lure a cat out with food, Hermes would have been the first out the door. But he's right here."

She lifted the sphinx in her arms.

"I don't get it," Peter muttered, running a hand through his hair. "What is going on here?"

# CHAPTER 5

## PINE GROVE CENTENNIAL PARK

It was another beautiful fall morning, although frost lingered on the ground. There was a nip to the air, but it quickly faded as the sun rose. Peter entwined his fingers with Jessica's as they walked through centennial park in the center of Pine Grove.

"I love this place," Jessica said, breathing in the wind.

"It's sure beautiful," Peter agreed.

The park had a small pond where ducks and geese liked to winter, fed by the people who came to the park and tossed out various grains, berries, and other tasty things. Several boxes were set up along the path filled with their feed and warnings that bread would cause the birds to be malnourished.

Sam tugged on his leash, whining as his head swung this way and that, searching the pond. Peter tugged lightly, bringing Sam back to his side. Jessica was walking a big Newfoundland dog that had surgery a few days ago. The large animal was gentle and welcoming to Sam, who had been nervous about her at first. They seemed to get along better now, though.

"Thanks for joining me on this walk," Jessica said. "Mindy needs to get moving more, and she just won't go for walks unless there's another dog with us."

Peter stroked Sam's head. "It's my pleasure. I certainly think Sam needs some more four-legged friends. I think he forgets he's a dog."

Peter wondered when Jessica would get to the real reason she had asked him specifically to come. They'd had little time to talk ever since their taco night. Peter still had little to share about the case. He was almost positive that Jessica was right and that something was going on. He just wasn't sure where to go from here, though.

"Do you want to get a cup of coffee and a late breakfast?" he offered. "We never got our lunch date."

Jessica laughed brightly. "Hey, but we had dinner. Doesn't that count as a makeup date?"

"Not when you have to make it yourself," Peter said wisely. He winked at her.

Jessica's cheeks turned pink, but she nodded.

They dropped Mindy off at the vet's office, and since Sam seemed to want to spend more time with the larger dog, they left him with her.

Peter and Jessica went to the café and took a seat on the patio.

"So," Jessica leaned her chin into her palm. "Are we going to get to the real reason you asked me to breakfast?"

"You mean the case?"

"You've been pussyfooting around it all morning," Jessica said. Her eyes twinkled. "Pun intended. But you've been waiting for me to bring it up, haven't you?"

Peter chuckled. Jessica could read him like a book. "Does Verna have any relatives in town?"

"She was never married, and the cats are her only children." Jessica tapped her fingers against the table. "I think she might have mentioned a nephew once or twice, but I don't really remember. From what I know, she didn't have any family at all."

"I see." Peter waved a server over. He was relieved to see it wasn't the same rude young man who had served them the last time they were here.

His mind turned over this new information. So, Verna didn't have any close relatives. That, combined with her cagey behavior when he asked her what work she had been in, showed something intense. Something that left her with either no time for a husband and children… or a job that made it unsafe for anyone to be in her immediate circle.

It was a sobering thought.

Peter pushed that thought from his mind, considering other options. "How did Verna get permission to have so many cats, anyway? I couldn't find any information about opening up a sanctuary in the middle of town as she has."

"What does that matter?" Jessica asked, her eyebrows furrowed.

"Well, if someone thinks she's mistreating them or is in a hoarding situation, they could steal the cats; I'm just trying to cover all the angles. She is an official sanctuary, isn't she?"

"Yes," Jessica snapped.

Peter held up his hands. "I'm not trying to accuse her of anything. I'm getting my facts straight."

Jessica sighed. "Sorry for my tone. Verna is a beautiful soul with a lot of heart and takes excellent care of those animals. But there are people in this town who are just… jerks."

"I'm sorry. I understand this has to be hard."

Jessica squeezed his hand. "Thanks for understanding. Yes, Verna is an official sanctuary. She was already established long before I came to Pine Grove. She's been having more problems since that new subdivision was built across from the cul-de-sac."

Peter made a mental note to check if any new neighbors had moved into the area in the last three weeks.

"Verna has to have a house inspection once a year to keep her status," Jessica said. Her eyes grew worried as she lowered her voice. "Her inspection is coming up; if the cats keep going missing, she might get closed down."

"Closed? But what will happen to the cats?"

Jessica shuddered. "Well, she can try to adopt them out. But they're all animals nobody else wanted. The chances are… they'll all be euthanized."

Peter's stomach clenched. There was more at stake than he had realized. *I have to figure this out and help Verna keep her sanctuary running. Otherwise…*

# CHAPTER 6
## MYERS RESIDENCE

Once he was home, Peter called his old colleague at the FBI, Tiff. She answered after only a few rings.

"Hey, Peter," Tiff greeted. "What can I do for you?"

"I need some information on a woman in town by the name of Verna Timms," he said.

There was a choking sound on the other end. "Verna Timms? Are you serious? Why?"

Peter was surprised that she knew the name, let alone sounding so shocked and awed. He frowned as he pinched his cell phone between his shoulder and ear. "Because she's involved in a case I've been asked to look into."

"Verna Timms... involved in one of your cases? Does that mean she lives in Pine Grove?" Tiff sounded excited now.

Peter grabbed the mail off his kitchen table, where he had left it. All bills. "I do not know what you're talking about, Tiff. Who is she?"

"Only the best of the best of the best in the agency," Tiff replied, sounding almost affronted now. "You worked for years; how did you never hear about her? She's a legend! A myth! An inspiration to half the junior agents who come in. She's been retired for something like twenty years, and her name is still spoken in hushed whispers."

Peter tossed the bills back on the table and moved to the fridge, checking the milk. "Sorry. She's not ringing a bell."

"Maybe this will. Ever heard of Shadowcat?"

Peter nearly dropped both the milk and the phone. He had to catch both, shoving the milk back into the fridge as he did so. He put the phone back to his ear. "Shadowcat? You're telling me that Verna Timms is Shadowcat?"

Tiff laughed, sounding pleased. "So, you have heard of her!"

"Of course!"

He had never met the agent whose code name was Shadowcat, but Tiff was right. She was spoken of in awe. She was well-known for her ability to slip in and out of seemingly impossible missions, with no one being the wiser. Rumor had it she had brought in more criminals than any other agent.

"And she's in Pine Grove?" Tiff asked again, sounding excited.

"Yes."

"But she's having trouble?"

Peter considered the situation. He doubted an agent like Shadowcat would want her dirty business broadcasted. "No, no. I just needed some information. This has cleared up a lot. Thanks, Tiff."

"Anytime."

Peter hung up and tapped his cell phone against his bottom lip, considering the situation. Knowing this, he had to get more information from Verna.

*I could have used this from the start,* he thought as he grabbed his keys. Sam was snoozing on the couch, and Peter left him there; he shouldn't be too long.

Was this Agency business? Had she talked to the people back at the Agency to tell them she might be targeted? If not, why hadn't she? If these disappearing cats were some sort of revenge, taking out her children, how was he supposed to figure it out?

He jumped into his car and headed back to town. He was going to get answers, one way or another.

⸫⟫✳⟪⸬

*The Timms Residence*

When Peter got to the cul-de-sac, it was dusk. A harsh wind blew in from the empty field, and Peter could already hear the yipping and howling of coyotes in the forest.

Verna's house was utterly dark. The screen door on the patio was wide open, and several cats were wandering down the stairs and back up, yowling and meowing in distress. Peter leaped from his car, his gut clenching. Something was wrong.

He hurried inside, finding the front door unlocked. He turned on a light, and all the cats that had been out on the porch streamed in. Their meows became more urgent. Peter shut the door and found the cat flap was locked.

Someone had driven the cats out and then locked them outside.

"Verna?" he called, heart hammering.

No response. Peter searched the house, but there was no sign of her anywhere. Out the back, the catio had had several screens ripped out. Peter shut and locked the cat flap that led out there. All the cats were staring at him, silent now.

The black cat, Hades, darted forward. He swiped at Peter's shoelace, then bolted for a doorway. He clawed at it, meowed loudly, and raced back at Peter.

Peter hurried over and opened the door. It led to a staircase going down into the basement.

And at the base of the stairs, in a crumpled, bleeding heap, was Verna.

# CHAPTER 7

## PINE GROVE HOSPITAL

"But my cats," Verna insisted.

Jessica, standing next to Peter, folded her arms. "No, you don't have to worry about them. I stopped in earlier and have already made sure they're taken care of for the night. You just worry about yourself."

Verna huffed. The bandage over her eyebrow had a small dark spot right in the middle, but luckily, she hadn't bled too much. Fortunately, she didn't have any broken bones. The doctors suspected she had a concussion. Since she was a little confused and disoriented, they kept her overnight.

Peter thought the staff would have to keep on their toes if they were going to keep her here. Verna was one stubborn woman.

Peter moved a little closer and touched Jessica's elbow. The last thing Verna needed was to be interrogated, but he still needed information. Convincing Jessica to help him had been difficult; in the end, though, she had agreed.

Now, she gave him a small, unhappy look. He nodded once.

Jessica squeezed Verna's hand. "Do you have any family I can call? You mentioned a nephew once, I think?"

"Oh, you don't have to bother him," Verna said quickly.

Peter leaned forward slightly. "So, you have a nephew?"

"Oh, yes. He's a dear, sweet soul. Few people can see that, though," Verna said sadly.

"Maybe I can call him, get him to stay with you?" Jessica suggested.

"No, no. He's a bit of a rough sort. He wouldn't exactly fit into a small place here in Pine Grove. My brother's son and my brother... well, he wasn't an exemplary parent. I tried my best to help my nephew out but there's only so much an aunt can do, especially when I was barred contact for years." Verna shook her head sadly.

Peter didn't like the sound of this. As her only living relative, this nephew had the potential to inherit everything. Could he have attacked her, wanting her house?

Verna's sharp eyes focused on his face. "Oh, no. I can see what you're thinking on your face. No, my nephew would never do something like this. He might have had it rough, but since my brother died, he's done his best to turn a corner. My nephew is a good boy if only he'd have the chance to prove it."

"Taking care of you while you're in recovery would be a chance," Peter pushed.

Verna shook her head. "No, no. He has a little bit of a temper, and with how the neighbors talk, he'd be bound to lose it." She mustered up a smile. "I will just get my things and head home."

"Verna," Jessica shook her head. "No. Stay the night."

"I don't have to do anything, young lady."

Peter ran a hand through his hair. "Jess, can I talk with her alone for a minute?"

Jessica hesitated. "Are you sure?"

"Oh, dear!" Verna gave a bright, hardy laugh. "Jessica, you don't have to worry over me. If Peter wants to speak with me, I will speak with him. Be a dear and get me a glass of water?"

Jessica didn't look very convinced, but she nodded. Before she left, though, she gave Peter a significant look. Even though they hadn't known each other for long, he understood it entirely.

Jessica was worried about Verna and didn't want Peter to push her too hard. Peter gave her a reassuring smile. During his years as a lawyer, he had learned how to gently interrogate a person to find what they were hiding without hurting them.

Once the vet was gone, Peter sat next to Verna's bed. "What happened?"

"I fell down the stairs. I've already told you that."

"I'm sorry, Verna, but I don't believe you." He kept his voice soothing. "I know you were part of the Agency. I know you took on tough cases and must have made enemies."

Verna shook her head. "I fell. That's all."

"When I came to your house, the cats were locked outside. You would never have done that." Peter looked deep into her eyes. "Someone pushed you, didn't they?"

"I…" Verna touched her forehead. "Oh, I'm so very dizzy. I can't—"

Peter held up a hand. "Please. I know when a person is faking an injury. That bump is real, but you're avoiding the question."

"Nobody pushed me." Verna dropped her hand, her kindly eyes narrowing. "I fell. That's all there is to it."

Was she protecting someone? Or was she trying to keep him out, so she could exact her own revenge against the perpetrator? Either way, Peter understood he would not get any more information.

He stopped by the water cooler to tell Jessica he was leaving and to ask her not to leave Verna alone. Jessica agreed.

Just as he was leaving the hospital, his phone rang. It was Tiff, and she didn't bother saying hello when he answered.

"Bad news," she said, sounding worried. "I looked into Shadowcat some more to see if I could find something. She worked on the McNulty case."

"McNulty?" Peter repeated.

"Francis and Felix McNulty were brothers. Verna brought them in and got them put away after she tracked down a lot of different crimes connected to them. Francis died only a few months ago, stabbed in the kidneys during a prison fight."

"And Felix?" Peter asked an uncomfortable feeling that he knew what she was going to say in his gut.

"He was released three weeks ago."

Right when the first cat disappeared. It seemed clear to Peter what was happening. Felix McNulty was out of prison… and going after Verna Timms for revenge.

"There's been a lot of calls made to her house," Tiff continued. "An unlisted number, but it's the same one every week, like clockwork. Maybe it's someone who knows what's going on?"

"Give it to me," Peter said.

One way or another, he had to figure this out. Before, whoever pushed Verna down the stairs tried to kill her again.

# CHAPTER 8

On Peter's way back to Verna's house, he called the number Tiff had given him. If whoever was calling Verna was harassing her, he had to find out who it was. The town was dark and dead at this time of night, without another car on the road.

The phone rang out until it hit a voice-answering message. No name was given by the robotic voice. Peter hung up and called again. This time, someone answered after five rings.

"What?" a male voice said from the other side, sounding irritated.

Wait, Peter knew that voice. Surprise rippled through Peter. He had to pull to a stop at the side of the road.

"If this is a prank call, you'd better pray I don't track you down," the voice warned.

Peter cleared his throat. "Marconi."

Silence answered him.

"It's Peter Myers."

"Myers?" Marconi's tone reflected the same shock Peter felt.

"Yeah."

Marconi whistled. "How did you get this number?"

"A friend let me know you have been calling a woman named

Verna Timms every week for a while." Peter's mind raced. Why would someone like Marconi be calling Verna?

Marconi was part of an organized crime family. Peter's father had worked as their organization's lawyer for many years, but Peter had wanted nothing to do with them. If Verna was getting threatening calls from these dangerous criminals...

Peter waited, but Marconi said nothing. Finally, Peter was fed up. "Have you been threatening her?"

"No."

Peter snorted. "Why should I believe you?"

"Hold on. I'm just making sure I'm alone." Another few moments of silence went by before Marconi sighed over the line. "Verna Timms is my aunt. I call her every week to check up on her and make sure she's doing okay. So why are you checking up on her?"

How much should Peter tell him? If Verna fell as she claimed... but no. It made little sense. Someone was going after her, most likely Felix McNulty.

"Someone has been stealing her cats. She asked me to figure out who. Today, I stopped by her house to find her at the bottom of her basement steps. I think someone pushed her."

"Is she okay?" Marconi asked, the worry clear in his voice.

"Yes. She's got a mild concussion, but the doctors think she'll be okay. I'm just trying to figure out who did this." Peter cleared his throat. "I have to ask—do you know she used to work for the FBI?"

Marconi snorted. "Of course I do. But you don't need to know more than that."

"You ever heard of Felix McNulty?"

"Yes. Why?" Marconi's voice was wary again.

Peter explained the connection between McNulty and Verna. When he was done, Marconi growled aloud. He was clearly furious. Peter could hear it in his voice.

"You think McNulty hurt my aunt?" Marconi asked.

"I don't know," Peter said. "It's a possibility."

"I'll look into it. And Myers? Thanks for letting me know."

Marconi hung up, leaving Peter uncertain. Did he do the right thing by telling Marconi? It was too late to change now. He continued, finally getting to Verna's house.

Every light in the house was on. Someone was inside.

# CHAPTER 9
## TIMMS RESIDENCE

Peter pulled the car up several houses away to avoid tipping off the intruder he was there. He called the police station, but the line was busy. Typical. Donnelly didn't have a proper reporting system. Whoever was in the house would be long gone before any of the inept police could get here, anyway.

There was only one thing for it. Peter searched his car for anything he could use as a defensive weapon but found nothing, not even a tire iron.

*I will have to make myself a kit for my car if I keep doing this,* he thought grimly as he got out of the car.

The blast of frigid wind hit him right in the face, stealing his breath. Ducking his head, Peter headed around the nearest house and crept through the backyards to Verna's house. The door leading to the catio was wide open.

*Intruder at Verna's. Call Donnelly,* Peter texted Jessica.

He turned the sound off his phone and slipped into the house. No cats came to greet him, but the loud sound of banging drawers and stomping feet came from above. Someone was on the upper floor, searching.

As Peter crept through the living room, he held in a gasp. The couches were cut open; vases and lamps were smashed on the floor. There were even holes punched into the walls. Whomever it was doing this wasn't just searching the house... they were ransacking the place.

Who would do this to a sweet old woman? Anger rose in Peter. Everything about this case made him angry. Verna was a good person who had dedicated her life to putting criminals away and only wanted to spend her golden years surrounded by the cats she so dearly loved.

She didn't deserve what was happening to her.

Peter headed up the stairs, sticking to the sides of the steps to keep them from creaking. When he reached the top, he pinpointed where the intruder was and charged. He smashed into the back of the intruder, and they rolled on the floor, fighting.

The intruder wore a hoodie and mask, with nylon stockings beneath the mask to hide their face. They punched Peter in the face. He tried to tackle back down but was distracted when he heard a plaintive meow from somewhere in the room. As his head turned, the intruder struck him again.

Darkness washed over his vision. The intruder threw him aside and raced away. By the time Peter returned to his feet and followed, they were gone.

He locked the doors and went back upstairs, following the meows. Soon, he found the cats stuffed into a small closet. They cried out and rubbed against his legs when he released them. Even the black cat, Hades, seemed happy to see him.

Peter counted them quickly. Eleven. That's how many Verna was supposed to have right now. Twelve would include the missing Persian, Persephone.

Peter pulled his phone from his pocket and sent a follow-up to Jessica. *Intruder gone. I'm staying the night here to clean up.*

*Okay. I'll keep trying to get hold of Donnelly.*

*Thanks.*

Peter sighed as he looked around. Well, better to start here. He grabbed a wastebasket off the floor and picked up the garbage. As he did so, he noticed a calendar on the floor. He picked it up, frowning at it.

Tomorrow's date was circled in red. Peter studied the calendar before putting it back on the wall where it began. He had a long night ahead of him.

# CHAPTER 10

## TIMMS RESIDENCE

It was almost noon when Peter was woken by a loud knock on the door. He groaned, covering his eyes to block out the sunlight. The last thing he wanted right now was to wake up.

The knock came again. Peter opened his eyes. For a moment, he forgot where he was. He seemed to have traveled back in time thirty or forty years. Something soft and warm curled up on his chest.

Right. He was at Verna's house, sleeping on the couch he'd pulled up from the basement. The old couch was a write-off, having been torn open so severely, but Verna had had a whole other entertainment setup in the basement.

More knocking, louder this time. The cats that had all piled up over him stirred. One of them purred right into his ear. He moved them aside as he sat up, yawning.

"I'll be there in a moment," he yelled.

The knocking stopped.

Peter searched for his shoes. He'd had a terribly long night. Donnelly had called him early morning to ask him about all the calls from Jessica but would not come out to check the scene himself.

Peter put his shoes back on and straightened his hair as he headed for the door. When he opened it, he found two officers from animal control on the other side, along with the woman sitting on the café patio glaring at Verna during his first meeting with her.

The woman's eyes widened in surprise. "Who are you?"

"Peter Myers," he said with a smile. "Verna Timms was hospitalized last night and asked me to watch her cats until she got out. Are you the inspection officers for the sanctuary?"

The two animal control officers glanced at each other. One of them cleared his throat. "Officer James here. I know nothing about a sanctuary, but we are here for an inspection."

Peter stepped back. "Please, come in."

The two officers came through. The woman, glaring at him, followed.

"And you're one of Verna's neighbors, aren't you?" Peter asked her politely.

The woman gave him a sneer and tossed her hair. "Mrs. Michelle Turner. What…"

As Peter led them into the living room, Michelle looked more shocked. Peter watched her closely.

Officer James scratched his head. "This isn't what we expected to find."

"Oh?" Peter picked up the sphinx cat and scratched its velvety skin. "What did you expect?"

"We were told we would confiscate neglected animals from a hoarding situation. But this place is amazing." Officer James looked distinctly impressed.

"They are neglected, and she is a hoarder," Michelle insisted. "This isn't what the house is supposed to look like. I mean, it's not what it looks like normally. He must have cleaned it up!"

"Verna has cleaners come in every day to help her," Peter said. "What did you expect? A house in utter disarray? Cat litter spread everywhere, perhaps? Or maybe you thought the catio screens would all be torn out?"

Michelle's face turned red as her hands tightened into fists at her sides.

Peter gestured around, turning his attention back to Officer James. "There have been some problems with vandalism in the backyard, but I can assure you, there is no hoarding here. Verna runs an accredited cat sanctuary and fostering program. She works closely with our local vet."

Officer James scratched his head, looking bewildered.

"I don't care if she's an accredited sanctuary!" Michelle burst out. She stomped her foot in a childish display. "I'm a member of the neighborhood association, and I don't care who thought that crazy old lady should have permission to have so many cats."

"She has the licenses she needs; all these cats would be put down if she couldn't take them in."

"I don't care," Michelle screeched. "She has no right to keep them! She can't even keep track of them! Three of the little beasts escaped from her. They're the reason she fell down her stairs."

Ah, just as he had thought. Peter leveled a glare at the woman. "I never said she fell down the stairs."

"I... I..." Michelle's red face turned ashen.

Peter pulled his cell phone from his pocket. "You made a big mistake here, Mrs. Turner. And I think Captain Donnelly will be very interested in learning just how you knew Verna had fallen down the stairs. In fact, I'm sure Verna will identify you. I'm sure she already knows who pushed her down those stairs."

"How dare you?" Michelle rasped, her eyes widening in terror.

Peter smiled at her as he plugged in Donnelly's number. "I hope you didn't hurt those cats, Michelle. It'll be much worse for you if you did."

The woman trembled, then turned to bolt toward the door. As she raced down the hall, Hades suddenly leaped from a shelf near the ceiling. He landed hard in the square of her back, knocking her down. Peter hurried over and pulled her to her feet, the two animal control officers close behind him.

"Michelle Turner," Peter intoned as he clasped her arm. "I'm placing you under a citizen's arrest."

# EPILOGUE
## TIMMS RESIDENCE

Winter looked like it was going to arrive sooner rather than later. Peter sat on the porch of Verna's house, a mug of coffee in his hand. Verna had returned home only a few minutes ago, but it wasn't Jessica who brought her home as Peter had expected.

The door opened, and Marconi stepped out. He sank onto a chair close to Peter and leaned forward, resting his elbows against his knees.

"You and the vet lady will keep an eye on my aunt, right?" Marconi asked, a jaded look in his eyes.

"If you don't feel comfortable hanging around," Peter agreed.

Marconi eyed him but nodded. "I don't want to get her into trouble by consorting with a known criminal. I imagine you'll be telling your FBI contacts as soon as I return your phone."

Peter couldn't help but smile. When Marconi demanded he hand over his cell phone, Peter had obeyed without question. It wasn't as though the local police would do anything about it. Besides, if Marconi was so worried about his aunt, he should be allowed to make sure she was okay.

"The FBI has to know that you're her nephew already," Peter said, lifting his coffee. "And though I'd love to know how someone with such strong ties to organized crime got her position, I have a feeling that's above my clearance levels."

"Bet your boots it is," Marconi actually smiled. "Aunt Verna is in her room upstairs with the cats resting. Doctors say she should stay on bed rest for at least two days and to take her back into the hospital if she shows any signs of getting worse."

"We'll keep an eye on her," Peter promised.

Marconi nodded. He sighed as he leaned back in his chair. "I found McNulty and made sure he knew my aunt was off limits. He will not bother her. But he knew nothing about the cats."

"McNulty wasn't behind any of this," Peter explained.

"But you said—"

"I know what I said. I hadn't gotten all the puzzle pieces yet, though."

Marconi tilted his head and arched one eyebrow. "But you have it now?"

Peter sipped his coffee.

"Is the threat over?" Marconi demanded, sounding a little annoyed.

"Yes. I'll tell you what happened, but you have to promise not to take things into your own hands."

Marconi nodded tersely. "If the threat is over, I won't do anything."

"It was a member of the neighborhood association. Michelle Turner."

"That batty woman?" Marconi's eyes widened. "I know my aunt complained about her, but… why?"

Peter had to smile, even though the situation was not at all funny. It really was a horrible series of events. "Michelle Turner has been trying to get Verna's license as a sanctuary revoked for years. She thinks the catio is an eyesore that brings down property values."

Marconi rubbed his temples. "And I guess she doesn't care that these cats wouldn't survive without Aunt Verna?"

"No. She's a classic cat-hater." Peter drank another gulp of coffee. "It seems she got fed up with it all and thought if she could make Verna seem incompetent, she'd lose the cats entirely. So, she broke the locks on the front porch to steal Ares and later grabbed Hera from the yard."

"And Persephone? She never left the house," Marconi asked.

"She took out the window screen and lured Persephone into a carrying case with a can of tuna. All three cats were found in her house a mile away. Luckily, they're all still healthy. Her husband apparently thought she was rescuing strays and took good care of them."

Marconi rubbed the back of his neck. "I kept telling her she could lock her doors, but she insisted that Pine Grove was safe and she didn't need to."

"Michelle took advantage of it. When she learned I was looking into the cats' disappearances; she decided she needed to take it a step further. She pushed Verna down the stairs, figuring it would look like she tripped over her cats." Peter glared at the cloudy sky.

He didn't understand how anybody could think so highly of themselves that they would do any of this. Pushing an old woman down the stairs only proved that Michelle was a pathetic excuse for a person.

"She's in jail now," Peter continued. "Donnelly's bringing up charges of attempted murder."

Marconi let out a shuddering breath. He turned to Peter, his expression one of pure gratitude. "Thank you. You saved my aunt's life. I owe you one."

Peter waved a hand. "Yeah, well. I'm just glad she's going to be okay."

"I mean it. I owe you." Marconi stood. "And maybe next time I'm around this way, I'll find a way to pay you back. See you around?"

He held out his hand to Peter. Peter considered the man before him before accepting the hand. "Take care of yourself."

Marconi grinned and headed out. Peter drank his coffee, thinking about Jessica with the cats at the clinic, about Sam waiting for him at home, and this case solved. And he thought about how he never imagined one day he'd consider Marconi a friend.

"Funny old world," he mumbled to himself. "Hilarious."

**The End.**

# A BAD EGG

## A MIKE AND MADDIE MYSTERY

# PROLOGUE

The handsomely dressed man swirled his glass of brandy, lounging on a leather chair as he watched the surveillance footage. It had been a long day with far too many hiccups. Sometimes he wondered why he was in this business. Sure, the pay was good, but he had to deal with such tedious problems…

A man came onto the screen, caught by the hidden camera. The viewer lowered his glass, scowling as the face of Josh Cardston became clear. The man just wouldn't give up, would he? At first, he'd been annoying, but now he was becoming a dangerous nuisance.

Something would have to be done about the Assistant District Attorney. While some ambition was admirable, getting in the way was not. Vancouver was a big place, big enough for them all to exist peacefully if people, such as Cardston, would just stick to their own lanes. It appeared some people had no sense of boundaries, though.

The man set his brandy down and turned off his video feed. He stood and moved to the window. The penthouse was well above the rest of downtown Vancouver, and a sea of stars lit the darkness of the night. He loved this sight, looking down on the world. It made him feel like a god, standing above all the little people down there who could only dream of the power he held, like a sword poised over their necks. He could bring that sword down at any moment, and it appeared Josh Cardston needed to be reminded of that.

The bright red and blue lights of some cop car flashed in the streets below, a reminder of the dangers of going after the ADA like this. However, Cardston had proven himself too dangerous an opponent to let him run about unchecked. It would have to be done carefully, though, to avoid the entanglement of the other cops.

No matter. The man stretched his arms over his head, then pulled out his cell phone. He'd get his best people on the matter, and within a month, Cardston would no longer be an issue he had to deal with.

For now, though, he could use some company.

"Hello, Ms. Moreau. I was wondering if you had time to spare to catch up with an old friend?"

# CHAPTER 1

Madeleine Moreau frowned at her cell phone as it rang again. She pushed her chestnut brown bangs from her eyes and declined the call. She turned the sound off her phone. Being home in Vancouver for the Easter holidays was a welcome return to her roots. But, goodness, she wished that Quinton Fresh would stop calling her.

Fresh lived up to his name. There had been a time when Maddie went giddy for his attention, but she wasn't a teenager anymore. From what she heard about Fresh these days, however, he had never matured past that stage of life.

Shaking her head, she opened her message thread to Michael Malison, her best friend and writing partner.

*The contest is about to start, and I'm turning the sound off my phone.*

She waited a moment, hoping that he'd respond but doubting that he would. Mike worked as a prolific ghostwriter who was always full of boundless ideas, and Maddie knew all too well how wrapped up he could get in his work. It was one reason they got along so well together.

She mainly worked as a professional plotter. Coming up with the plots others could use was something she adored; creating characters and dreaming of all the mischief they could do was her passion. Some she loved too much to sell, and those she kept for herself.

Though writer's block sometimes hit the best of them, even Mike had dry spells despite seeming perfect in every regard.

Right now, though, he was amidst a truly stunning adventure. Maddie was excited to read the final project. She itched to be at her computer herself but had promised her parents that she wouldn't spend the entire visit chained to the desk.

And so that was how she ended up at this Easter Egg decorating contest. Her parents were off socializing, and Maddie knew most of the surrounding people. After all, she had run in these circles growing up... and she wouldn't trust any of them as far as she could spit. Not that a lady would spit in this company. She could only imagine the scandal that would ensue if she did.

With a chuckle, Maddie headed for the table her parents had bought for the family. She was looking forward to this, even if she had forgotten how much she hated being stuck in high society. Even though she had recently felt sorry for herself because she hadn't accomplished her childhood dreams, she was more than happy with the life she had created for herself in Coeur D'Alene, Idaho.

"Why, is that the Moreau's oldest girl?" a voice called out, clearly trying to catch her attention.

"I believe so, Mother," another voice said.

Maddie had turned her head automatically before she recognized who it was. She instantly regretted it, as she could no longer pretend she hadn't heard them. Instead, she put on a false smile as Judy and Jacob Cardston approached.

*Weirdly, father, mother, and son all have the same initials,* Maddie thought. Judy, a woman with striking red hair and eyes as sharp as her tongue, stopped before her.

"My dear, don't you look well?" Judy purred. She was, as usual, decked out in pearls and gold.

The Cardston family was very proud of the father, Josh, as the Assistant District Attorney. Still, they were quite gaudy about flashing around their wealth accumulated by the son's deals in the oil business. Maddie would have felt sorry for them if they weren't such acerbic people. They wanted to be part of 'high society,' but they didn't have the respectability that allowed them anywhere but tagging along at the fringes.

*Although,* Maddie mused, *that's just one more thing I dislike about 'high society.'*

She put on her most friendly smile as she nodded once at Judy. "Thank you so much, Mrs. Cardston. I'm very pleased to see you here as well. Will Mr. Cardston be joining us?"

Judy waved her hand. "Joshie is just so busy with that big trial with the drug cartel—"

"Now, Mother," Jacob chuckled, glancing around nervously. "We don't want to bore everyone with details of that horrible business. Ms. Moreau, will you be in Vancouver long?"

"Just the weekend," Maddie replied.

Jacob sidled a little closer, grinning widely, making Maddie very uncomfortable. "Perhaps I can convince you to stick around for a little longer? After all, since you had a headache the other day when I called—"

"I'm afraid not," Maddie interrupted. "I'm not sure if you have heard, but I am working closely with a... well-known figure," she blurted. Playing undercover was her favorite part when she and Mike helped their friend Carson solve cases. Now was a perfect place to pull that out again. She glanced around furtively. "My client would not wish for me to delay."

She had found that hinting at something secret was enough to make many people change their tact. A few would insist on knowing, but she always had the excuse of not being able to disclose anything. As it was, being so close to secrets satisfied most individuals.

Jacob, however, didn't seem to be much deterred. "Surely, an exception can be made? You could tell him you have family affairs to attend to."

"I'm afraid—" she started but was cut off.

Jacob stepped forward, too close. He opened his mouth and—

Maddie sighed in relief when the master of ceremonies stepped up to the mike and called for attention. How did everyone around her seem to know she was still single? It constantly felt like she was deflecting unwanted attention.

*At least this is a charity event;* she thought as she took her seat at the table again. Her parents made their way back toward her.

She peeked at her cell phone one last time, hoping to have a message from Mike. Her heart jumped to her throat when she saw she did. She skimmed it.

*Call me when you have free time—I have exciting news!*

Maddie couldn't help but chuckle. What exciting news would this be? Mike could be a bit dramatic, but she loved spending time with him. Rarely was she ever bored with her friend in her life... something she was intensely grateful for.

"What is that smile for?" her mother, Katherine, teased, taking a seat beside her.

"Nothing," Maddie replied. She sat through the master of ceremonies' opening remarks, only truly paying attention once the rules were explained.

"All eggs are raw and must be emptied before the painting can begin," he declared, his voice booming to the corners of the lavishly decorated hall. "You have been provided with the tools needed to blow them out, but also know this—the eggs must not go to waste. Every bit must be eaten before you paint. If you wish, you may cook them first, but you will be docked points."

Maddie felt herself turn a little green at that. The thought of eating raw eggs never sat well with her.

Beside her, her mother clapped her hands. "All right, so once we have half a dozen eggs blown out, I'll start drinking them," she said, a gleeful look in her eyes. "I've been practicing."

"I just don't understand how you can do that," Maddie's father said, looking as green as Maddie felt.

Katherine grinned. "Oh, Henry! I do it with ease, of course!"

"You have five minutes," the speaker said, "and then we will begin!"

"Five minutes," Maddie groaned. "Here I hoped that we'd get started already. I've already sorted out our paints and other supplies and organized them for optimum usage."

Her parents gave each other sly grins. Katherine looped an arm through hers and pulled her to her feet. "Well, I suppose we have just enough time to introduce you to Ben Hiddlestone, then."

Ben Hiddlestone? That was a name Maddie didn't know, but it tickled a recognition in the back of her brain. Was it a family who had moved back to Vancouver after leaving? She had to admit; she was curious to find out who this man was.

She wasn't fond of her mother's obvious ploy, though. All the same, she knew when to be polite and put on a smile as they approached a nearby table.

"Mr. Hiddlestone," Katherine trilled. "I'd like you to meet my daughter, Maddie. She's a writer like yourself."

The man at the table looked up. Maddie's heart jumped to her throat; Ben Hiddlestone! Now she knew that name. He was the author of a prolific mystery series that had taken the world by storm. She hadn't read any of the books but had watched the recently produced TV series with Mike and Carson.

Ben had deep, clear eyes, a stunning shade of blue. He got to his feet and shook Maddie's hand. "Nice to meet you, Maddie."

"You as well," Maddie said, trying to keep her cool. "But please don't like my mother's introduction fool you. I have some modest success with my writings, but I do it mostly for myself."

"If you write, it makes you a writer," Ben replied swiftly, the crooked grin on his face making Maddie's heart race.

She couldn't help but laugh. "Yes, I agree with you on that point. So, Mr. Hiddlestone—"

"Ben, please," he said.

"Ben. How long are you in town?"

# CHAPTER 2

Before Ben could reply, the chime indicated the contest had begun. Maddie frowned, but when Ben took his seat, she was pleased to see that he was at the table next to her and her parents.

Katherine scooted closer to Henry, giving Maddie a clever sort of grin. Maddie almost rolled her eyes, but she was too grateful. Usually, her mother's meddling in her life was unwelcome, but Ben was an interesting sort, and Maddie found herself grateful.

*Oh dear,* she thought as she took her seat, *Mother will never let me down.*

Her father pricked a hole in the top and bottom of the eggs, leaving her mother to blow out the insides and gobble them up; Maddie cleaned the delicate shells and set them to dry.

"Are you fine conversing with the enemy?" Ben asked her, also cleaning the eggs for his table.

"Of course," Maddie teased. "I am always interested in a good enemy redemption story."

Ben grinned at her. "To answer your question, I've been in Vancouver for a good year now. I didn't intend to move here. I never thought I would enjoy living in a city, but this place grabbed a firm hold of my heart, and I simply can't leave."

Maddie carefully cleaned out the first eggshell she was given, ignoring the sounds of her mother slurping up the raw egg.

"It's certainly vibrant," she agreed. "So many people with unique experiences. So much culture and centers where you can learn and grow."

Ben nodded, setting aside his first egg. "I will say, though, one year isn't long enough to meet many interesting people."

Maddie kept her smile on her face, but it was only polite. She viewed Ben with a new, guarded look. The thing she hated most about the society and culture was the tendency to write off people as non-interesting simply because they weren't wealthy or hadn't had the training in the unspoken rules of said culture.

"What, in your opinion, makes a person interesting?" she asked. "I have never found Vancouver lacking in that respect."

Ben hummed. "Indeed, Vancouver is not the one that is lacking. You might not realize, but I'm painfully shy. People only become interesting once I build up the courage to speak with them. For instance, you're an interesting person, Maddie, because I have strung my words together without scattering my thoughts across the floor like beads off a broken necklace."

Maddie laughed.

Ben grimaced. "I'm talking too florid, aren't I?"

"Not at all," Maddie assured him. "In fact, you are quite charming. I will have to keep my guard up. Otherwise, you will distract me from my task, and my team will fall behind."

"Then I must be more charming to distract you," Ben replied with a grin.

Their attention was drawn to the Cardston table, where Judy had gotten to her feet, holding her stomach. Jacob was busy cleaning the eggs, apparently not noticing or not caring that his mother looked in distress.

Ben jumped to his feet. "Mrs. Cardston, are you all right?"

Judy plastered a smile over her face. "Yes, yes. I'm fine. I'm afraid I drank some milk this morning before I realized it had gone off. It seems it's catching up with me, combined with these raw eggs. If you'll excuse me."

She hurried toward the lady's toilet. Madeline winced as she followed Judy with her eyes. It certainly was never pleasant to be caught with such difficulties in public. She searched in her purse, thinking she might have something she could offer the older woman.

"So, Maddie," Ben said as he resumed work, "what sorts of things do you write?"

Maddie looked up. She had met other authors in the past who looked down on what she did for a living and hoped Ben wouldn't be one of them. But then, if he was going to think less of her for it, it was best to get it out in the open immediately so as not to waste her time.

"Whatever strikes my fancy, more or less," she replied. "What I write, I write for myself and then self-publish once it's to my standards. I do well, but where I mostly shine is the plotting. I freelance for other authors who are having a hard time."

"Plotting?"

Maddie nodded. Her parents were nearly through all the eggs now, leaving her needing to catch up with cleaning. "I get bored with writing, to be honest. I mostly enjoy creating characters and plots. Of course, I work based on my client's specifications, but that makes me the happiest."

Ben glanced at his own pile of eggshells building up. "I see. I couldn't do that myself. Plotting is the hardest part for me. I will spend months on an outline, agonizing over every little detail. I can't write without it, though."

"I know a few people like that. My partner, Mike, can pull a whole novel out of a single sentence without planning, but I don't understand how he can do it."

"Your partner?" Ben asked, seeming a little deflated.

At first, Maddie didn't quite understand why he would be disappointed to hear that. Then it occurred to her that he thought she was speaking of a romantic partner. Her cheeks turned pink as her eyes widened. Was she reading too much into this, or was Ben Hiddlestone interested in her?

"My business partner," she said, watching him closely.

His face brightened, and her cheeks grew hot as her blush deepened. He leaned forward, his job forgotten. "Business partner?"

"Yes, in a manner of speaking. Mike has also succeeded in self-publishing but enjoys ghostwriting for other authors. I will often create the plot, and he'll write it. I must admit, he's a much better writer than I am." Maddie smiled as she thought of her friend. She wished he could be here with her; he'd have so much to say to Ben.

"If he's so good, why does he write for other people rather than himself?" Ben asked with a furrow in his brow. "I couldn't possibly. I will not put in the work so that someone else can get the credit."

"It's what he enjoys," Madeline shrugged.

Ben returned to cleaning off the eggshells. "I suppose that's as good of a reason as anything. My goals in writing must differ from his or yours. There's nothing wrong with that, is there?"

"Certainly not. If we all had the same goals, the competition would drive us to extinction."

Ben chortled. "I have never heard it said that way."

By this time, Jacob Cardston had already finished blowing out the eggs. He set the raw eggs aside, looking peeved as he peered at the lady's washroom. He grunted and painted the shells.

Maddie remembered how she had been looking for something for Mrs. Cardston and turned to her parents. "Can you clean up the shells for a bit? I'm going to see if Mrs. Cardston would like an antacid or something."

"I'll come with you," Katherine said, pushing from the table. She turned to Henry. "Is that all right?"

"Certainly, certainly," Henry replied. The eggs were emptied at this point, and he moved to Maddie's seat to continue the cleaning.

As they headed for the lady's washroom, Katherine slipped her arm into Maddie's. "So? You and Mr. Hiddlestone seem to have had a lively conversation."

"It's an interesting conversation, at least," Maddie agreed. "Though all we have talked about so far is work."

"Start somewhere," Katherine said, squeezing her daughter's hand.

Maddie smiled briefly as she swiped her chestnut-brown hair out of her eyes. Ben Hiddlestone sure was an interesting person. His genre wasn't one of Maddie's favorites. But now that she had met the man, she thought it might be prudent to check one of his books out from the library. She might not be in town for long, but it was always a good idea to have connections.

However, this wasn't a conversation she wanted with her mother. Not that Katherine was overly meddlesome in most instances, but she had a rather strict idea of how a young woman should live her life... and being single at thirty years old wasn't exactly following that path.

When they entered the lady's washrooms, it was oddly quiet.

"Mrs. Cardston?" Maddie called.

"Judy?" Katherine said.

An odd sort of feeling crept over Maddie. No sound came from any of the stalls; each one shut as though someone might be inside. She tentatively pushed open the first door, finding it empty.

"Maddie," Katherine said a little nervously. "Don't you think—"

"Stay here, Mother," Maddie said. She moved to the next stall and pushed it open. Empty. So were the third and fourth stalls.

Katherine seemed to get even more agitated. "She probably went back to the competition, and we just missed her."

The fifth and last stall in the washroom was locked. Madeline knocked on the door. "Mrs. Cardston? Are you in there? I have some Pepto Bismol that you could take for your stomach."

No answer. Bracing herself, Maddie crouched and peered beneath the door. Her heart slammed into her ribs, and she covered her mouth with her hand, shooting straight up. She whirled, turning to face her mother. Katherine's face was pale.

"What is it?" she asked in a trembling voice.

Maddie lowered her hand and straightened her shoulders. "Call 9-1-1. We need the police here immediately—I think Judy Cardston might have been murdered."

# CHAPTER 3

Mike's stomach dropped as he approached the community hall where the egg-decorating contest was to occur. Police cars and an ambulance sat near the entrance, all flashing lights. He glanced at Detective Carson Luttrell and hurried his steps.

Inside the hall, they found a group of well-dressed people talking to one another in low voices. Various police officers were in the room, getting their statements. Mike knew all too well how the procedure happened. As he searched the crowd for Maddie, Carson headed toward one of the few men wearing a business suit. Mike followed; though he wanted to find Maddie, he also didn't want to end up having to search for both.

"Detective," Carson greeted with a nod. "I'm Carson Luttrell, a detective with the Coeur D'Alene police department."

"Coeur D'Alene?" the strange detective looked Carson up and down before nodding. "Ah, yes. I read about you in the paper. You solved a few rather large cases of gem smuggling. I'm Luke Jameson. What can I do for you?"

There was a certain guardedness in the way the detective spoke. Mike closed down his automatic thoughts on why that would be—

while indeed there were juicy options for the man's jaded response, it didn't matter at the moment.

"What's happened?" Carson asked.

"A woman was found dead in the toilets. My ME's preliminary investigation suggests she was poisoned. The victim was seen leaving the room with stomach pains shortly before she was found dead," Detective Jameson folded his arms.

Carson drew a hand through his curly, dark hair. "I recognize that I have no jurisdiction here in Canada. But if I can be of any assistance, please let me know."

"Thank you. I'm not sure what you can do, though… after all, as you said, you have no jurisdiction."

Mike bit the tip of his tongue to stop laughing. Was it professional jealousy? Was that why Detective Jameson was being so cagey?

"My friend Mike here and I are looking for another friend of ours, Maddie Moreau," Carson continued. "She said she was going to be here. Would you know where she is?"

The detective's frown deepened as he looked between Mike and Carson. "Yes… she's over there with her parents," he nodded to a table and chairs behind the police line. "She and her mother found the body."

Relief swept through Mike as he finally caught sight of Maddie's chestnut hair. He left the two detectives and hurried toward her. She had an arm around the older woman, which must be her mother, but she suddenly looked up as though she could sense Mike's approach.

Her eyes widened, and she hurried over toward him. As soon as they reached one another, Maddie threw her arms around him.

"What are you doing here?"

Mike hugged her back tightly. "Carson ended up having an international conference here in Vancouver, and I came along to surprise you. Are you all right?"

Maddie nodded slowly. She released him and stepped back, letting out a shuddering breath. "I think so. I will be, at least. As many times as I have seen dead bodies while working with Carson on his cases, I never thought I'd be the one to find the body of someone I knew. Judy was lively and sociable, and then…."

She shuddered. Mike put his arm around her again. "It's going to be okay."

"I... I know." Maddie managed a small smile and guided Mike back to where her parents were waiting. "Mike, I'd like to introduce you to my mother, Katherine, and my father, Henry."

"Pleased to meet you," Mike said. "I just wish it were under better circumstances."

"I saw you were talking with the detective," Henry said without so much as a hello.

Katherine turned big, watery eyes toward him. "What did he say?"

"Preliminary findings are that Mrs. Cardston was poisoned," Mike said carefully. He didn't want to share too much of what the two detectives talked about. He glanced around the room, noting the dozens of eggs lying about.

Maddie nodded. "I thought so. She showed the signs. I also smelled something nutty in the eggs she had been eating before the police collected them for evidence. I guess cyanide was somehow introduced to the eggs; she had been eating them before she suddenly went to the washroom, clutching her stomach."

"Do you have to talk about it?" Katherine moaned.

Maddie turned to her mother. "Yes, I do. Mike and I have worked with Carson—Detective Luttrell—for many years now. I can understand if you don't want to hear us discuss the case, given what happened... it's just easier if I try to put emotional distance between the victim and me."

Mike almost thought Katherine would cry, but she only nodded once; she and Henry excused themselves, leaving Maddie and Mike alone. A sudden loud cry from the doors made them both turn.

"Oh dear," Maddie murmured, putting a hand on her chest.

Two new men had joined Detective Jameson. Carson was nowhere to be seen, but these two men hugged each other. One of them seemed to be on the verge of falling over. Mike touched Maddie's hand and gave her a quizzical look.

"The older one, wearing the blue shirt, is Josh Cardston. Judy's husband," Maddie whispered, nodding towards the man slowly slumping toward the floor. "The older one is his son, Jacob."

"Jacob seems to take it well," Mike murmured.

A voice spoke behind them. "I've spent some time with the Cardston's these last few days and concluded that the son has had to raise his parents emotionally. This would just be another example—him needing to comfort his father while his grief is ignored."

Mike turned, and shock flooded him when he saw who it was. Despite the situation, all he could do was stare, tongue-tied. Over the last few days, he'd read not one but three of Ben Hiddlestone's books, unable to put them down—and here the author was in the flesh.

Luckily, he didn't need to think of anything witty to say. By this time, Carson had joined them.

"Luttrell," Ben said, his brows arching in surprise. "What an unexpected pleasure!"

"Hiddlestone!" Carson eagerly shook Ben's hand. "It's been too long. Last I heard, you were out in LA. What brings you to Canada?"

"Research for a new book," Ben replied without missing a beat.

Mike choked on his surprise and coughed.

"Easy," Carson said, patting his back.

Mike shook him off. "You never told me you know Ben Hiddlestone!"

"You never asked."

"Why would I?" Mike shot back. "Am I supposed to ask you if you're the son of a Transylvanian vampire? No, because it's not something a normal person thinks about!"

Carson laughed and patted Mike's shoulder. "Easy, there. Yes, I know Ben. We met a few years back while he was writing his first book. A first book I hear did very well," Carson added with a smile to Ben.

Ben grinned back. "You and I will have to get together to catch up, Luttrell."

"Of course."

Carson looked at his two younger friends, and his expression sobered slightly. "In the meantime, I should get Maddie and Mike to somewhere we can talk. Maddie, where are your parents? I rented a minivan; I have room for everyone."

They moved off, though Mike kept throwing glances over his shoulder. Ben Hiddlestone!

Katherine and Henry both thanked Carson for the offer of a ride but assured him they had their own transportation; they invited Mike and Carson to their home for the evening, to which Mike looked to Maddie. Her expression was neutral as she shook her head.

"Maybe tomorrow," she said. "For tonight, I'm certain that Mike and Carson want to get to their hotel. You did say something about a conference you were attending?"

"Tomorrow," Carson said.

"Then perhaps Mike and I will spend time while you're busy with that." She turned back to her parents, smiling now. "I'll just go with them to make sure they can find the hotel. I'll get a taxi back home. Okay?"

Looking at her, you'd hardly know that anything was amiss. Mike knew her too well to believe that, though. Her parents were fooled entirely or excellent actors themselves. They kissed her cheeks and told her to tell them if she'd be home after dark.

Maddie was quiet on the way to their vehicle, and Mike also fell silent. Carson talked about the conference he was attending to fill the space left by them. As he continued talking as though nothing had happened, Mike felt a suspicion entering his mind.

Once they were at the hotel, Maddie ordered some pasta. The hotel room Carson had been given for the conference had been no good, on the other side of town and would have meant a long drive every day. So, he and Mike had shared a room closer to the conference location and Maddie's home.

The room they'd ended up with had two queen-sized beds sitting snugly against a wall, an enormous TV screen, a mini fridge, and little else. It was not exactly the grandest of rooms, but it was comfortable enough for them.

"This isn't like a case in Coeur D'Alene," Carson said abruptly when the pasta arrived. "We are not to go getting involved. Allow the police here to do their jobs, all right? I don't want you getting involved in something that could put you in danger."

Mike rolled his eyes. "Yes, Dad. But really, how come you never told me about Ben Hiddlestone? And, for that matter, why was he at an egg decorating contest?"

Carson shook his head, rolling his eyes upward as though asking for strength.

Maddie giggled for the first time at that. "It was a charity event. He must have been there to support the charity."

"Ah." Mike let it drop because Carson seemed to want him to. But he couldn't help but think… was that all there was to the story? Or was there more that Carson wasn't saying?

# CHAPTER 4

Detective Jameson looked less pleased when he was welcomed into Maddie's family room. Well, it was her parent's family room, but the detective wasn't there for them. They weren't even home, having gone to an Easter celebration in another part of town. Even a murder couldn't stop their social lives.

Maddie and Mike were catching up on the conference notes that Carson had taken for them during the day when the detective arrived. He brought with him a copy of the ME's report.

"I hope you understand this is a courtesy because your parents have been so generous in supporting the Vancouver Police Department," the detective said severely, a glimmer in his eyes stating that he wasn't happy about this at all.

"Thank you, Detective. I appreciate this more than you know," Maddie said in response. She gave him one of her most winning smiles, imagining herself as the innocent main character in a story full of intrigue and mystery. "I hope it wasn't too much trouble."

The detective seemed a little mollified but didn't protest when Maddie, Mike, and Carson went through the file. After a moment of reading, Maddie looked up at Detective Jameson.

"There was cyanide found on the *outside* of all the eggs?" she asked incredulously.

"Yes," Jameson said. "We—"

Maddie's phone rang, interrupting him. She dug it from her pocket. "You've got to be kidding me! Ugh, this man will not leave me alone."

Mike held his hand out, and she handed it over to him. He frowned. "Who's Quinton Fresh?"

"He's a flat-out jerk that doesn't know how to take no for an answer," Maddie seethed, folding her arms. "We met when we were teens at a dance, and he likes to harass me whenever I come back to Vancouver."

"I think he's only looking for a booty call; he never contacts me unless I'm in town, and then it's all, 'Oh, how about you swing by my place for a movie.' No matter how many times I tell him to leave me alone."

Mike answered the phone, ignoring Maddie's hiss. As he snarled into the phone, he put on a deeper voice, "Leave the lady alone."

Then he hung up.

Maddie stared at him. She'd never known him to act so toughly before! He chuckled and handed the phone back; a flush rose in her cheeks. "With any luck, that will keep him off your back."

"For a little while, at least," Maddie said. She smiled at Mike, pleased; if she remembered Quinton Fresh's character correctly, he was only intimidated by other men.

She smiled at her friend before turning back to Detective Jameson. "Pardon my manners, Detective. You were saying about the poison?"

Jameson squinted at her suspiciously. "All the shells tested positive for cyanide. Apparently, Jacob Cardston was poking holes in the ends and handing them to his mother to blow out and eat; then, he would clean the shells. Trace amounts were found on his hands."

"But how could there be enough on the shells to kill her?" Maddie pressed. "Wouldn't she have smelled the cyanide? I could smell it on her."

"Egg shells are highly porous," Jameson replied.

At this, Mike nodded. "It's for exchanging oxygen; you can smother or drown an egg because of it."

Jameson turned his frown to Mike. "Yes, exactly. The concentration of cyanide found inside the eggs is at much higher concentrations than on the shells. Neither Jacob nor Judy have a genetic condition that impairs their sense of smell. Those who sat around them assumed they had almond-flavored coffee."

"I see. And then when Mrs. Cardston consumed the raw eggs...." Maddie shook her head. "She never stood a chance, poor woman."

"But it still begs the question, why would anyone want to kill her?" Mike asked.

Detective Jameson opened his mouth, but Carson spoke first. "Didn't I tell you two not to get involved in this case?"

Both Maddie and Mike ducked their heads.

"You'll have to forgive them, Detective," Carson said to Jameson. "Maddie and Mike here often step in to help me in Coeur D'Alene. In fact, they were vital in arresting those jewel-smuggling rings you mentioned when we first met."

Jameson hummed, rocking back on his heels. "I see. So, you have some experience working with the police in an unofficial capacity?"

Maddie leaned forward. Something in the way he spoke showed that there was more to the question than simple curiosity. She studied the detective as he and Carson viewed each other. It was as though they were having a silent conversation, and Maddie had to wonder how they were already so in tune with one another.

*Is it a detective thing? Or do they know one another more than they're letting on?*

Eventually, Carson nodded once as though he was consenting to something. Maddie glanced at Mike, seeing the same excitement in his eyes that was growing more in her.

"There is something else you might do for this case, Miss Moreau," Detective Jameson said. "You see, we have reason to believe that Judy Cardston was targeted by organized crime; Josh Cardston is the ADA and has been working nonstop to collect enough evidence to charge the ringleader."

Maddie perched on the edge of her seat, nodding. She felt that if she pushed too much, Jameson would change his mind about whatever he planned to ask of her.

"Quinton Fresh. We believe he has used his wealth and position to start a rather prolific crime organization. Josh is far too distraught to continue his investigation, especially since it could have easily been both his wife and son killed in this attack," Jameson continued. He adjusted his cuffs, looking a little reluctant.

Maddie's stomach plummeted. "Oh, dear. So, you're saying that you want me to get close to Quinton to get information from him?"

"In a manner of speaking, yes. There is a... undercover officer that has been tasked with the job. However, getting a meeting with Fresh has proven impossible." Jameson looked even more reluctant to continue. He glanced at Carson once more.

"Is there something between you two?" Mike asked suddenly.

Carson arched a brow as he turned to Mike. "What do you mean?"

"You keep looking at one another as though you've made a previous agreement. Is there really a conference in town?" he demanded, standing now.

"Why would you think there isn't?"

"Carson, it was your idea that we come to Vancouver in the first place. It was your idea to surprise Maddie. I thought nothing of it, but why would the police department in Coeur D'Alene send you to Vancouver? In a completely different country?" Mike folded his arms as he narrowed his eyes at their older friend. "Or is there another reason?"

Jameson chuckled.

Maddie looked between the two detectives, and a sense of betrayal washed through her. It passed soon enough, though, and she burst out laughing. What a great joke! "So, you brought us here to help the Vancouver police to solve a crime?"

Carson stood. "I'm sorry for the deception, Maddie, Mike. Detective Jameson and I have known each other for many years. He reached out to me after hearing about our success with those smugglers in the States. I agreed to help, provided the two of you stayed out of it."

"Why would you want us to stay out of it?" Maddie demanded. "Haven't we proven useful in your cases?"

"Major crime in a big city like this isn't like in Coeur D'Alene; it's tough, dangerous. More competition means more ruthless criminals. I didn't want the two of you... well, I think you both know what you can often do." Carson gave them both pointed looks that made Maddie feel like a rebellious teenager rather than the thirty-year-old she was.

She nodded meekly. Oh, she knew exactly what he was talking about. Though Carson was a dear friend and would often come to them to muse over a case, he was also something of a big brother figure. Maddie didn't have any older siblings, just one younger sister. She imagined Carson would be what a brother would be.

Detective Jameson watched the exchange with some amusement. "And what are they like?"

Mike waved a hand. "Oh, it's just that we tend to let our imaginations run away with us from time to time."

"Carson was probably afraid that once we found out everything, we would plot out the murder like a storybook." Maddie paused, and a wicked grin spread over her face. Just as her younger sister loved to torment her, she loved to tease Carson. "For instance, I could say that Quinton Fresh is secretly in love with Josh Cardston."

"Oh, that's good," Mike said. "And he built up a false narrative in his head, thinking that Cardston loved him too."

Maddie nodded. "But as the ADA cracks down on his case against the criminal mastermind—"

"The illusion is broken," Mike finished.

"He concludes it's the woman's fault," Maddie said, annoyance tinging her voice again. "After all, he's just the sort of misogynist that will do that."

Mike agreed. "So, he takes out the wife, certain that once she's out of the way, his illusion will return. And in the meantime, he pursues the young woman he has been obsessed with since childhood—"

"Please." Maddie held up her hand, grimacing. "That's far enough. It's all well and good doing this sort of conjecture when we don't know the players but talking about people whose faces I know is a different matter—especially when one is my own!"

Carson sighed loudly. "And this is exactly what I was afraid of. Now. If you're done making up stories?"

"We are," Mike said with a pleasant nod.

"Then I have a task for you, Miss Moreau," Jameson said, focusing on Maddie. "And I'm afraid it will have some risk associated with it."

Maddie nodded once. She was perfectly fine with taking some risks. "Give me the job. I'll do the best I can."

# CHAPTER 5

Maddie twitched, nervous as she waited at a steakhouse on Carrall Street. It was a pricy restaurant, just the sort a man looking to impress a lady would make a reservation at. *Or,* Maddie mused *the other way around.*

Of course, neither she nor the man she was going to meet—Quinton Fresh—had chosen the location. No, it was decided on by none other than Detective Jameson. After all, this wasn't a date; it was a sting. Maddie wasn't entirely sure how she was supposed to help the police in this case.

Well, that wasn't entirely true, either. After all, she was supposed to get Quinton here. The undercover officer Jameson had mentioned they contacted her and used this opportunity to get close to Fresh. With any luck, that meant he would interrupt the situation before she had to actually converse with Fresh…

That seemed more dangerous than any other undercover mission she'd had before. Not that she thought Quinton would now pull out a gun and wave it in her face. Because she might just drop dead from sheer boredom.

She hoped that her undercover contact would get here soon,

though. She needed to know what she had to do when Quinton arrived.

"Well, hello! Maddie, wasn't it?" Ben Hiddlestone slid into the chair next to her.

Maddie jumped. She flushed slightly as she took in the dark blue suit he wore. He looked extremely attractive, that was for sure. "Um, yes. Mr. Hiddlestone. I didn't expect you to be here."

She swallowed, glancing around. What would the undercover officer think if he showed up to find her already occupied?

"I like to check out the fine dining establishments from time to time," Ben replied, reaching across the table to touch her hand. "It's research for my new book—The Dove Dies at Dawn."

Maddie's breath caught. That was the code she'd been given to know the name of her undercover contact! She forced herself to breathe in, calming herself and smiled. She was good at this; playing a role was her favorite part of doing this sort of work.

She could do this without tipping Quinton off what was happening.

"What's this book about?" she asked, keeping her tone cool.

"It's a crime novel. I'm stuck on a certain spot, though. As a plotter, maybe you can help? My heroine is setting up the villain, trying to get him and the hero alone together somehow." Quinton rested his elbow on the table. "I'm just not sure how she will do it."

"I see," Maddie glanced over his shoulder; Quinton had arrived and was currently searching the restaurant. "The problem is, your hero and heroine don't have time to devise a plan, do they?"

Ben straightened. "Exactly. The tension is rising, and the hero wants to ensure his lady love is out of danger before anything happens to her."

He gave her a significant look. Maddie waved to Quinton, not to let him know where she was so much as to let Ben know he had arrived. She put on her angriest face as she turned to Ben. Quinton was heading their way at this time but was too far to hear them.

She ducked her head, making sure he couldn't read her lips—which she doubted he could, but it was better to be safe than sorry.

"Your heroine is going to help your hero bond with the villain. Nothing better to talk about than an irrational woman, right?"

"I wouldn't—" Ben started.

But Maddie surged to her feet. "How dare you! You misogynistic brute! I'm so sick of men who think they can just waltz into my life and demand my attention. You're just like him!"

She threw her arm out to full length, pointing accusingly at Quinton. He stopped, his eyes widening as she picked up her glass of water. Ben yelped as she dumped it over his head, and Maddie threw her hair over her shoulder, grabbing a second glass. She turned to Quinton, who tensed.

Maddie drained the glass in one swallow and threw it to the floor, shattering it—she would have to come back and apologize to the staff and pay them a tip once this was over.

"Why is it that I invite one man here to finally get him off my back only to be accosted by another absolute—I can't even say it!" She grabbed her purse and tucked it under her arm. "Never call me again, Quinton Fresh. And as for you—" she snarled as she turned to Ben. "I hope you rot!"

Maddie stormed off, pushing past Quinton as she did. She was already at the door by the time the hostess and manager got onto the floor. As she threw her weight onto the door, popping it open, she heard Quinton in the back.

"Women. There's no knowing what's going to set them off, is there?"

She smiled as she hurried to the car, where Mike and Carson were waiting for her. She slid into the front seat and quickly buckled up.

"I think it worked," she said as Mike pulled out from the parking spot. "At least… I hope it has."

⟫⟩✷⟨⟪

The next day, Maddie was taking a walk along the beach, enjoying the mild spring morning, when Ben Hiddlestone suddenly fell in step next to her. Maddie jumped but quickly relaxed. She gave him a puzzled smile.

Ever since the bizarre happenings of the previous night, she had been pondering over what role Ben Hiddlestone had in all of this. She remembered how Carson had known him that day when Judy died, but how did that end up with Ben being an undercover police officer?

"So... you are an author, right?" she finally asked, glancing at him.

Ben smiled. "I am. And I'm sorry to have taken you by surprise. People know of my connections to law enforcement, but only so because it helps to research my writing. If they knew exactly how connected I was, I'd never be able to get close to the people I need to get close to."

Maddie hummed. She and Mike had been up most of the night creating elaborate situations in which Ben's role played center stage. "And what sort of people do you need to get close to?"

"People like Quinton Fresh. As an author, I can get close to people who would never allow the police near them. It works especially well when the mark is a fan of my work," Ben grimaced. "But Quinton would never see me. He's too full of himself to be in the presence of anyone who might draw more eyes than him."

"You have that right," Maddie agreed fervently.

"So, I must thank you for your aid last night," Ben continued, turning his face to the pale sky. Gulls wheeled and sang while the rolls of waves crashed onto the sand. "And more than thanks, Maddie. I was able to get close enough to Fresh to clone his phone and bug his home. Nobody else has ever gotten close enough... we'll know soon if he ordered Judy Cardston's death."

Maddie sighed in relief. It was a great boon to know that. Poor Judy hadn't deserved what happened to her, no matter how tacky and arrogant she had been. "Do you think the police will arrest him soon?"

"I can't comment more on an open investigation, you know that," Ben teased. He bumped her lightly, grinning.

"Of course." Knowing he couldn't say it, though, didn't ease the burning curiosity in Maddie's gut. A chill wind picked up, and she stuffed her hands into her pockets to warm them. "Can you give me a hint?"

Ben chuckled. "Perhaps a little one… if the police find so much as a drop of cyanide in Fresh's apartment, the Assistant District Attorney will bring the might of the law down on him."

"And with good reason. I can't imagine what pain Mr. Cardston must be going through, having lost his wife like that."

"I'm certain something will turn up," Ben said bracingly.

Maddie nodded. Quinton had always struck her as the arrogant kind. Ever since they first met, he had thrown money around as though it should be enough to get anything he wanted. He'd always had his circle, people he knew would never betray him because he pay rolled their entire lives.

Some might say that money didn't buy loyalty, but Quinton Fresh certainly didn't hold to that belief.

"Cardston will get what he wants," Ben said, his voice firm. "Quinton may have temporarily won relief, but he doesn't know what he did. I've never seen a man so determined before. I can't help but believe that Quinton made a grave mistake."

"Even if they find the cyanide, they won't know how he tainted the eggs," Maddie said. "There has to be something else, something we are missing."

"What, though?"

Maddie shook her head. She had no idea how to answer that. What, indeed?

Her phone buzzed, and she dug it from her pocket; it was Mike.

"Get back quickly," Mike said as soon as she answered. "I have the answers!"

"What answers?" Maddie asked at once. Mike loved to be dramatic. And asking questions to which she already knew the answer was one way Maddie supported his dramatics.

Mike's voice was high with delight. "The case, Maddie! I have the answers to the case!"

# CHAPTER 6

Mike was pacing back and forth in the hotel room by the time Maddie and Ben arrived. His eyes lit up when he saw the famous author, though he attempted to keep calm. It wasn't often that he could show off in front of someone he had such admiration for.

"Mr. Hiddlestone, I'm glad you're here," he said, extending his hand.

"Ben, please. And I couldn't resist! Tell me, how did you break the case?"

Mike glanced at his phone. "We should wait for Carson and Detective Jameson; they will arrive here shortly. If I'm right—and let's face it, I'm only wrong about twenty percent of the time—we will have an arrest by the end of the day!"

Maddie sat down. "Very well. Let's wait."

"Aren't you going to ask?" Mike pushed.

"You said we should wait, and so, we should wait," Maddie replied, smiling sweetly at him.

Ben leaned against the wall, looking between them with a half-smile on his face. "Why does it feel like I'm witnessing a ritual?"

"Because you are," Maddie said swiftly. "We do this all time."

"I see."

Mike had to chuckle; he had to admit it was a little silly. But it was also great fun. "Please don't let it put you off our methods. We have, after all, managed to resolve some very serious cases."

Ben waved a hand. "No, no. Of course not. I'm actually finding it very interesting. I would never have guessed that you were a couple at first. But now that I see you interact more, it's quite obvious."

"A couple?" Maddie repeated.

"We're not a couple," Mike said. He glanced at Maddie, his brow furrowed. "Right? I mean, we do work together and often eat together."

Maddie's expression changed, a light pink color rising in her cheeks and over her freckled nose. "If we have to ask, it means we're not a couple."

"I suppose!" Mike laughed as he turned back to Ben. "There, you see? We're not a couple."

Ben looked bemused. "I don't see... but I suppose it's just one of those mysteries, eh?"

"I suppose," Maddie repeated.

The door opened, admitting the two detectives. Mike smiled to see Carson's usual expression, trying to be stern but secretly amused. Jameson just looked plain confused. Suddenly, Mike felt a little nervous. One new person was simple enough to absorb into their normal routine, but two?

"All right," Carson said as he sat on one bed next to Maddie. "So, what have you figured out?"

"The eggs didn't kill her," Mike declared. He picked up the ME's report, flipped it open to the toxicology report, handed it to Jameson, and then found the report on the eggs. "There was a higher concentration in the eggs than in her system. I've been researching all morning; if she ingested any of those eggs, she should have had a higher amount in her system."

Jameson frowned as he checked over Mike's notes. "I thought there was something wrong with this."

Mike nodded, puffing out his chest. "Knowing that, I phoned the ME and had them run tests on the victim's stomach contents. They found no cyanide in those eggs. So, I had them check her body more carefully, and they discovered a small needle mark between her toes."

"She had a head injury, but we assumed it was caused when she fell," Ben said.

"I believe that the killer planned to poison her with the eggs. But they realized they had a better chance when they saw her enter the toilets." Mike walked back and forth, explaining his thoughts. "They followed her in, clubbed her over her head, and took off her shoe to inject the cyanide directly into her system."

Maddie and Carson listened with strict attention.

Mike paused and turned to his audience with a flair. "Then they put the cyanide in the eggs and on the shells afterward, during the chaos."

"Who was the killer, though?" Maddie asked, sitting on the edge of the bed. "Why would they need to remove the woman's shoe, inject her with the poison, and then put it back on her? Then poison the eggs?"

"We know who it was, Quinton Fresh," Jameson protested.

Mike shook his head slyly. "Quinton Fresh wasn't at the contest. He paid someone to do it."

"Who?"

"Someone who spilled cyanide on his hands when he killed Judy and had to cover it up somehow. Someone who simply didn't know what he was doing because he never had to think for himself before."

"Oh, no," Maddie breathed. "You don't mean… her own son? I never even noticed if he left his table!"

"Something he was counting on. After all, nobody cared about Jacob Cardston. They only cared about his father. He doesn't even have his own bank account; he was living off his parents still."

Jameson was silent as he processed this information. "You're saying Jacob Cardston murdered his own mother?"

"That's what I'm saying," Mike replied grimly. "And he's not the smartest man. Otherwise, he would have planned the murder better."

"It fits," Ben said as he pushed from the wall. "I'm sure with the bug I planted in Quinton's apartment; we'll be able to get the evidence we need."

Mike nodded. "He'll have paid in cash; find the cash, and I'm sure Jacob Cardston will tell the truth."

*»)᛭᛫᛫(«*

It took less than a day for Detective Jameson to find the money Quinton Fresh gave Jacob Cardston. It was a severe blow to Josh to learn his own son had murdered his mother. He confessed quickly, even admitting that he was supposed to kill Josh instead of Judy. But Jacob thought Quinton would take the fall and killed his mother, who had always controlled him.

Maddie sat with her legs curled under her, wearing an oversized shirt as she listened to Detective Jameson explain it all. She shook her head sadly. "To think it was all over greed."

"It's tragic, but thanks to you and Ben working together, we finally found the evidence we need to put Quinton Fresh behind bars. And he thinks it was Jacob who planted those bugs." Jameson shook his head, a grin tugging at his lips. "It almost seems a shame we have to protect the lout. But letting Fresh kill him would be ethically wrong. He'll serve his own jail sentence."

"And that is all we can hope for," Mike agreed.

Maddie chewed her lip as she stared into her coffee mug. It was good to have yet another case closed, although it was undoubtedly a shock to her parents when she admitted what part in solving it she had played. She had told them about the cases in Coeur D'Alene, but as it turned out, they thought she was exaggerating.

The question remained in her mind, though… no matter how much she tried to push it aside, she couldn't stop wondering why Ben Hiddlestone had thought she and Mike were a couple.

*Some mysteries aren't supposed to be solved,* she told herself firmly as she stood.

"Thank you for letting us know, Detective. If there's anything else, we can help you with—"

"I'll contact Carson," the detective replied.

Maddie smiled and headed into the kitchen. She didn't feel much like finishing her coffee. Too much caffeine. Maybe some nice soothing tea…

Once in the kitchen, her phone dinged. She pulled it out, and her heart fluttered, seeing it was from Ben.

*I'm heading to the aquarium. Would you and Mike like to join me?*

Maddie grinned as she typed back. They had already been planning to visit the Vancouver Aquarium. *We'll meet you there.*

*Isn't this great?* She thought as she poured out her coffee. *Mike is going to be thrilled.*

Her smile only grew wider. Yes, she was looking forward to going home, but this had been a better Easter than she expected. Apparently, eggs and chocolate weren't the only things she found!

**The End.**

# DISCOVERED ON EASTER

## A JANE AND KENNEDY DANIELS MYSTERY

# CHAPTER 1

"Kennedy! Kennedy! Come quick!" Jane screamed as she paced back and forth in the bathroom.

Kennedy ran up the stairs, her heart pounding, assuming the worst.

"What's wrong? What happened?" Kennedy panicked.

"It happened. It finally happened!" Jane croaked, tears of joy welling in her eyes.

Kennedy looked back at Jane, searching for answers before her eyes fell on the positive pregnancy test in Jane's hands.

"You're pregnant?" Kennedy gasped, her heart pounding so hard she could hear it beating in her ears.

"I'm pregnant," Jane nodded.

"We are going to have a family?" Kennedy welled up, a lump in her throat.

"It finally happened. We are going to be mums," Jane flung her arms around Kennedy.

Everything they had ever wanted was now within their grasp. It had been a long and emotional journey, but the end was near – the day when Jane and Kennedy got to hold their child in their arms.

With their history of finding trouble around the holidays, the rest of the year was spent being extra cautious. No trips abroad, no galas with the mayor. Instead, Jane and Kennedy spent the next eight months plan-ning and decorating the nursery in neutral colours. Kennedy even grew fond of shopping with Jane. Naturally, they shopped for baby clothes, and Kennedy was determined to find the right gadgets to help the baby.

They had decided not to find out the gender; they wanted it to be a surprise. Each ultrasound picture was framed and made into a collage in the nursery; a wall dedicated to the journey of becoming parents. Jane and Kennedy marked off the calendar each day as Jane's due date approached at the start of April.

"What do you think of the name Chandler if it's a boy?" Jane asked.

"I thought we decided not to name him or her after our favourite TV show characters," Kennedy chuckled.

"Okay, then, what names do you like?" Jane asked.

Hours had passed before they had settled on one, laughing at each other's choices of names and competing over who could come up with the funniest name. The perfect name for if it was a girl or a boy. Morgan.

"Morgan, I love it," Jane smiled, hugging her enormous bump.

⦅⦅⦆⦆✳⦅⦅⦆⦆

With Jane being due any day, Jane and Kennedy decided to stay close to home for Easter. In previous years, they had taken turns spending the Easter weekend with their parents; one year heading to Surrey to see Jane's family, the following heading to the States to visit Kennedy's. Not wanting to take risks, the Daniels invited their closest family and friends to their house for Easter this year.

Jane was finding it increasingly harder to walk with her large bump taking over her petite frame. So she sat at the table and spent weeks designing and decorating the perfect Easter invitations to occupy her mind. Kennedy had insisted a phone call would have sufficed, but Jane was insistent. An invitation was something the family could keep as a keepsake, not just of the night, but as a reminder of when their child was born.

"Hon, I'm sure our families will never forget the year our child was born," Kennedy teased.

"I'm fat, swollen, and practically bedridden for the next few weeks. Please let me have this one thing to stop me from going insane," Jane complained.

As the final weeks of her pregnancy approached, Jane was becoming irritable. She tried her hardest not to snap, but Kennedy found it amusing and teased Jane at every turn. Eventually, Jane realised it was Kennedy's way of showing her just how strong she was, and Jane appreciated her more for it.

"You drive me crazy.... but I love you for it," Jane winked, tossing a scrunched-up piece of paper at Kennedy after she made another joke about swollen ankles.

"I love you too, babe. Now rest those feet; I'll bring you a cup of tea."

When Kennedy returned with the tea, Jane had finally put the finishing touches on her invitations.

"How does this sound?" Jane asked, passing Kennedy the invitation.

The small square card was decorated like the cover of a murder mystery novel. It reminded Kennedy of one of her favourites, Agatha Christie's *Poirot*. The main difference was that Jane had subtly slipped baby chicks, bunnies, and easter eggs into the design. It was pretty clever and stunning. Written in the middle of the invitation in beautiful cursive gold writing read:

```
To all, beware. This Easter dinner will
    not all be as it seems. Mystery will
    be the Piece de Resistance at the end
    of the Easter festivities.
```

"I think it's beautiful. But you know your mother will hate it. She hates surprises," Kennedy warned as she helped Jane pack the invitations into envelopes.

"She will be fine," Jane shrugged.

True enough, a few days later, when the invitations reached their recipients and the RSVPs came in, Kennedy strolled in with a smirk.

"Hi Leslie, yes, she's here; hold on,... it's your mum," Kennedy grinned, handing Jane the phone.

Jane tapped the loudspeaker button and smiled, "Hi Mum, how are you?"

"Don't give me that; what is this invitation? You know I don't like surprises. How am I supposed to enjoy dinner knowing something is going on? I will be on edge all night," Leslie complained down the phone, making Jane and Kennedy laugh.

"Oh, come on, Mum. What's the worst that can happen?"

»»)»*«(««

"And what sort of mystery would you have us solve? What is wrong with a good old-fashioned Easter egg hunt?" Leslie groaned into the phone.

"Easter egg hunts are for kids, Mum. We are hosting a murder mystery dinner," Jane replied.

"Of course you are. You girls are something else," Leslie chuckled. "You know I'm not the only one who doesn't like surprises," she insisted.

"I know, Mum, but Rochelle and Ben haven't complained. On the contrary, they are looking forward to it."

Kennedy rolled her eyes at the mention of her parents' name and headed to her office. Rochelle and Ben were known for their competitive nature, a trait shared by Jane's mother, Leslie. Kennedy knew Jane was trying to rile up her mother to convince her the dinner would be fun.

"Oh, Rochelle and Ben are coming?" Leslie asked.

"Of course! What sort of wife would I be if I didn't invite my in-laws?"

"Oh no, it's not that.... I suppose it will make the festivities different, and it could be fun. Will there be teams? What's the set-up?" Leslie asked.

"Oh no, Mum, I'm not giving you any hints. You will have to wait for the dinner party like everyone else," Jane laughed.

Leslie was a stubborn woman and kept pushing for hints, but Jane wouldn't give up.

"You will be my death," Leslie laughed, hoping her choice of words would jolt Jane into giving something up.

"Well, we won't know that until we draw names from the hat, will we?" Jane chuckled, ending the call.

Jane waddled across the house to Kennedy's office, where Kennedy was hard at work coding a new program for a client. She worked hard for weeks, and the deadline was approaching. It was one of Kennedy's more complex orders, and Jane knew she had been struggling with it.

"How's it going?" Jane asked, placing the phone back on the receiver.

"Fine, for now anyway. The next phase will be the make-or-break; the client's requests are quite unique. I want to get it done before our dinner party and Morgan's arrival," Kennedy sighed, rubbing her hands over her face.

Jane waddled over and started massaging Kennedy's shoulders; she could feel the tension through her fingertips.

"You will be fine, honey. I believe in you," Jane kissed Kennedy's cheek.

"Thanks, babe. What can I do for my beautiful wife?"

# CHAPTER 2

Easter was always a hard time for Detective Arthur Gottfried. He never told Kennedy or Jane, but ten years prior, his wife of twelve years had passed at Easter time. Arthur still blamed himself. He had been working on a tough case and drinking so he couldn't drive. Laura had been out with friends and struggled to get a ride home. Her taxi had been involved in a crash, and Arthur lost the love of his life.

"I still blame myself. If only I hadn't been drinking, I could have collected her; she would still be here," Arthur confessed to Dannie.

Arthur and Dannie had been dating for over a year, and Dannie was the first person since Laura that Arthur felt genuinely comfortable with. They had been discussing moving in together, so Arthur thought it was time to share his past with her.

"Arthur, it wasn't your fault. How do you know if you had gone to collect her, the two of you wouldn't have been involved in the crash? It's something out of your control, and I'm sure Laura wouldn't want you spending your life blaming yourself for it," Dannie comforted.

"I've never told anyone else about Laura. Jane and Kennedy don't even know about her," Arthur confessed.

"I'm truly honoured that you feel comfortable enough to share this with me," Dannie smiled.

"Why wouldn't I? I love you, Dannie," Arthur grinned.

"I love you too, Arthur," Dannie said as she kissed Arthur softly. "Speaking of Jane and Kennedy, a letter came from them today." Dannie handed Arthur the decorative envelope.

Opening it and quickly reading, Arthur burst out laughing. Then, shaking his head, he picked up his mobile and dialled Jane's number.

·))》✻❅《((·

"Good morning, Arthur; how are you and Dannie?" Jane chirped.

"Wonderful, thank you. We just received your invitation. What spectacle do you have planned now?" Arthur chuckled.

"Oh, you know, a little murder mystery. Why not change things up a bit? Solving a crime around a celebration seems to be mine and Kennedy's thing. This time, I thought, why not control the fun myself?"

"Well, Dannie and I would love to come. Thank you for the invite," Arthur smiled, taking Dannie's hand.

"Wonderful," Jane cheered.

Dannie took the phone from Arthur and talked with Jane about how her pregnancy was going and about baby names. In the year since Dannie and Arthur reacquainted, Jane, Kennedy and Dannie had become quite close. The Daniels liked Dannie very much and found she brought out a happier side of Arthur; they loved seeing Arthur happy.

"I can't wait. What wine should I bring?" Dannie asked.

"You have great taste in wine; I'll let you pick."

"And I'll bring something equally as tasty and non-alcoholic for you to Jane," Arthur chirped, feeling slightly left out of the conversation.

"Wonderful, see you both soon," Jane ended the call.

·))》✻❅《((·

Two days before Easter, Jane began to prepare. First, with Kennedy's help, she set up a speaker in the loft space that would alert the guests with screams of terror, letting them know festivities were about to commence when Kennedy pressed the button on her phone. Next, they scattered clues around the house and linked up speakers around the house.

"Have you figured out who the killer will be yet?" Kennedy asked.

"If I'm honest, I haven't even figured out who the victim will be," Jane admitted.

"Well, you better hurry up. The dinner is in two days."

Jane wanted every part of the property to be involved. So, clues were hidden around the kitchen, lounge, everywhere except Kennedy's office – for obvious reasons, and even the garden.

"Kennedy, can you help me with this?" Jane asked, dragging a box in from the hall.

"Jane, what are you doing? Don't be dragging anything heavy. What is it?"

"It's a scarecrow I ordered to play the victim's body. I know our mothers wouldn't be happy if they pulled out the victim's name and had to sit the rest of the game out, so...."

Kennedy ripped open the box and immediately jumped back. The scarecrow had come from a website dedicated to murder mysteries, and the prop didn't disappoint. The scarecrow was dressed in a dinner suit with fake blood drenching its once crisp white shirt. The face looked almost human, with soft to the touch skin – An expression of horror and wide eyes depict the look of lifeless eyes.

"Jane, that's terrifying," Kennedy gasped, clutching her hand to her chest.

"I know it's great, isn't it? And it was cheap, a discontinued line."

"I can see why," Kennedy laughed, scooping up the fake body and flinging it over her shoulder.

"So, where is he going?" Kennedy asked.

"The garden shed, between the wheelbarrow and the potted plans."

"I just hope none of the neighbours are looking out their window; otherwise, they will like we have killed someone if they see me trudging this thing across the lawn," Kennedy laughed.

∙⫸⟫❊⟪⫷∙

On the morning of the Easter dinner, Jane began her day by preparing the vegetables she would cook later. With the vegetables prepped, she started blending her secret basting mixture; even Kennedy didn't know the list of ingredients. Then, scoring the lamb, Jane rubbed her secret recipe into the meat before popping it into the oven to slow roast for the rest of the day. Jane's lamb was famous throughout the family. It was always so tender and juicy that it fell clean off the bone.

"I definitely smell garlic and rosemary," Kennedy said, popping her head into the kitchen.

"I'm still not telling you my secret recipe," Jane teased, washing her hands.

"You are going to have to tell me one day."

Jane shook her head and playfully stuck out her tongue, making Kennedy laugh.

"Jane, there is something I have been wanting to ask you for a while now, but I'm worried about the answer," Kennedy said, keeping her eyes cast down.

"What's wrong, honey? You know you can ask me anything," Jane said, waddling over to Jane and taking her hands in hers.

"It's nothing too big, just a concern of mine."

Jane was beginning to panic; she and Kennedy had never had issues communicating. What could have Kennedy so concerned?

"Baby, talk to me," Jane worried.

"It's just about dinner, the murder mystery thing…...please tell me you haven't got us costumes," Kennedy mocked, her act breaking as she began to laugh.

"Oh, Kennedy, you are so mean. I was so worried for a second. And to answer your question, no, I haven't, but I wouldn't say no to getting dolled up. It's still a family occasion, after all."

"Of course," Kennedy kissed Jane before heading upstairs.

Jane had thought about making the event a fancy-dress party, getting into the whole spirit of a good murder mystery. But when she couldn't find a suitable costume for herself, given her huge baby bump, she decided against it. She didn't want to be the only one not dressed for the occasion.

Instead, she opted for a simple black floor-length dress, flat sandals, and accessories with gold jewellery. Kennedy had opted for a teal suit with a white shirt; she looked beautiful.

The guest list consisted of Jane's parents, Kennedy's parents, Arthur and Dannie, Jane's cousin Lucia and a few other relatives and friends from college. Jane couldn't wait to see everyone again; she hadn't seen Lucia before she was arrested on Boxing Day. It had been even longer since Kennedy had seen her parents other than via a computer screen. Jane and Kennedy had been so busy travelling to Italy to return the stolen jewels, Kennedy's near miss on Halloween and then Jane breaking her leg. Then, with Valentine's Day the year before marking their first steps to getting pregnant and Jane studying for her private investigator licence, life had got in the way of family visits. With a new addition to the family only days away, it was the perfect time for a family get-together.

# CHAPTER 3

A row of cars lined the street outside Jane and Kennedy's home – Cars of all shapes, sizes, and vintages. Classic cars were a long-lost hobby of Arthur. So, when his eyes fell on a cherry red 1957 Jaguar Roadster, it took all he had not to geek out. He wondered whom the car might belong to. Eyeing all the cars was a welcome distraction from the nerves bubbling in his stomach. But he didn't have time to study the cars. They had a dinner date to attend.

"Arthur, are you okay?" Dannie asked as Arthur stood outside the door, hesitant to ring the doorbell.

"I'm just a little nervous. I don't really know anyone except Jane and Kennedy. I wonder what their families are like; I heard stories, but…."

"You are not alone. I'm here with you. Come on, ring the bell," Dannie urged softly.

Arthur stood a little taller, nodding and smiling back at the woman he loved before pressing the bell. As Dannie and Arthur stood waiting, it was evident that the line of cars belonged to the many voices inside the house. Roars of laughter and chatter could be heard even through the thick wooden door.

"Arthur, Dannie, it's so good to see you. Sorry it took so long to answer. As you can see, it's getting harder and harder to move around," Jane laughed, rubbing her round belly.

"Wow, Jane, you look ready to pop," Dannie joked, making Arthur's face erupt in horror, only to make the women laugh harder.

"Any day now," Jane ushered the pair inside.

The house was full of people gathered, chatting and laughing. Some Arthur recognised from pictures around the Daniels' home. Kennedy joined her wife in greeting Arthur and Dannie before taking them around the house and introducing everyone.

"Arthur, this is my mother, Leslie and my father, George," Jane introduced. "Mum, Dad, this is Detective Arthur Gottfried and his girl-friend, Doctor Danielle Fitzpatrick."

"Please, call me Dannie," Dannie smiled, shaking Leslie and George's hands.

"Pleasure to meet you both. We have heard great things about you, Detective Gottfried. You have quite the fan club with my daughter and daughter-in-law," George boasted.

"That's so kind, but I am a fan of theirs. They are wonderful people," Arthur smiled back, blushing slightly.

Arthur had never been one to accept or give compliments easily. Dannie gently squeezed his hand, letting him know everything was okay. She had positively influenced him, opening him up to new things and letting his softer, gentler side come to the surface.

"The first course is almost ready if everyone would like to take their seats," Jane chirped, leading everyone into the dining room.

ᐅᐳ❊❬❬

The dining room was decorated in shades of white, dusky pink, and brown to match the clues and decorations scattered across the table. The long dining table was big enough to fit sixteen guests, covered in a white lace tablecloth with a dusky pink chiffon runner down the centre. Candles of all shapes and sizes were scattered in the middle of the table, mixed with mystery-themed props. Magnifying glasses, white cotton gloves, a monocle, and a tobacco pipe were just a few decorations sitting pride of place. Still, as it was an Easter celebration, Jane had also included small mini easter eggs, figurine bunnies, and chicks scattered throughout the room. On each place setting was a napkin wrapped in red ribbon with an envelope with the word *clue* written in gold ink.

Each place setting had each person's name. To throw everyone off the scent and get everyone to know each other a little better, Jane had purposely split couples up and mixed the families in the seating arrangements.

"What? I'm not sitting with your father?" Leslie groaned.

"Come, Mrs Devon, it shall be fun," Arthur chimed, pulling out Leslie's chair for her as his name was next to hers.

"Don't worry, Leslie, I'll keep an eye on George for you," Dannie teased, winking at Arthur taking her seat next to George.

"Where are we sitting?" asked Rochelle, Kennedy's mother.

"Next to me," came Lucia's voice.

It took a while for all the guests to find their assigned seats. Jane and Kennedy allowed everyone to finish their drinks and aquatint themselves before filling their glasses and serving the first course, which Rochelle had graciously provided. Bistro salad with goat's cheese croutes. Everyone had come prepared with some dish to help take some pressure off Jane, leaving her to spend her time on the main course and the mystery games for the evening.

"Wow, Rochelle. This salad is delicious," Leslie chimed.

"Thank you, it's so simple, really. It's a goat's cheese base with fresh lettuce, my special secret mixture of herbs and a homemade mustard vinaigrette. I fell in love with the recipe when I studied in Paris," Rochelle explained.

"It will pair nicely with the wine Yvette brought," chimed Jane's cousin Amanda as she handed Kennedy the bottle of Sauvignon Blanc.

"So, when does the mystery start?" George asked, eager to get involved.

George was probably the most competitive member of the group. He had been itching to open his clue since he sat down, but Leslie had given him a glare telling him to wait until everyone else opened theirs.

"While I clear up the first course, everyone, feel free to read your

clues. But remember, don't share the details with the other players,"
Jane winked.

∞)》✻〈(《

"Oh, how exciting. I will admit, I wasn't too enthused about a
murder mystery dinner. But Jane, you have done such a wonderful
job, and this clue intrigued me," chimed Kennedy's old college tutor,
Mrs Tree.

Mrs Tree had always been known for being outspoken. She cared
little for what people thought of her and always encouraged her
students to speak their minds freely. "Nothing ventured, nothing
gained. Regrets form by unspoken words and plans not put into
action," was her catchphrase.

"Shush, Andrea, don't give anything away," nudged her husband,
Ronald.

"Oh, don't be silly, Ronald, as if I would ever let a thing slip," Mrs
Tree waved dismissively.

As the quests chatted amongst themselves, Jane and Kennedy
beamed with pride. This was precisely what they had hoped for. The
perfect blend of their family, enjoying each other's company before
Morgan made an appearance. Seeing the mix of people, personalities,
and viewpoints that would influence their child warmed the heart.
Wisdom from generations; it took a village to raise a child, and the
Daniels were ecstatic with the village of people they had in their
corner.

Jane grabbed Kennedy's hand, placing it on her stomach as little
Morgan kicked away.

"Morgan can feel the love from everyone too," Jane whispered.

"He or she can't wait to meet her family. He or she knows how
much love awaits," Kennedy kissed Jane's head softly.

Jane had prepared two cocktail menus as some of Jane's cousins
were under eighteen. One for the adults and one that she and the
younger guests could enjoy.

"Oooh, can I have the basil and lime lemonade?" asked Lucia.

"Sure, I'll join you. Any other cocktail requests?" Jane asked the room.

"What's the easter bunny cocktail?" asked Kennedy.

Jane had changed her mind about the drink menu so many times over the previous days that some of the cocktails were a surprise to her too.

"Oh, it's beautiful. I found the recipe online. It's got a kick to it, so don't drink too many. It's vodka, chocolate liquor, cherry brandy, and chocolate-flavoured sugar syrup. But I also add a splash of blackcurrant liquor," Jane beamed with pride at her creation.

"You are trying to get us all drunk, aren't you?" laughed Ben raising his glass of whiskey.

"Well, if I can't drink, I just want to make sure everyone else has fun on my behalf," Jane joked.

»»۵⚹۷﹐««

With her father's help, Jane brought the lamb to serve at the table. George insisted his daughter sit down and allow him to carve while Kennedy brought out the honey-roasted Gammon and began to carve. A delectable combination of smells filled the room; mouths watered as everyone passed around the serving plates, selecting their chosen vegetables. Jane had thought of everything. The main course consisted of Jane's famous glazed slow-cooked lamb, honey-roasted Gammon and slow-roasted beef. There was a selection for everyone. She had also prepared salmon for her cousins, who had recently shifted to a pescatarian diet and vegetarian options of aubergine, courgette, and asparagus for some of the other guests, along with mashed, boiled, and roasted potatoes. The guests were spoilt for choice. Jane had also prepared Yorkshire puddings, a mix of herb-roasted vegetables, stuffing, and gravies.

"Wow, Jane, you really have spoilt us. This food is delicious," Dannie smiled.

"Well, I wanted today to be special," Jane beamed.

As the guests tucked into their food, Jane grew even more

emotional. Flooded with joy, love, and gratitude, she couldn't keep it to herself any longer. Pushing her chair back, she stood with tears in her eyes, tapping a spoon to her glass to draw everyone's attention.

"Sorry to interrupt your meal, but I have a few things I want to say," Jane began.

Reaching for Kennedy's hand, she looked at her wife with a heart filled to bursting.

"Kennedy, you have given me more than you will ever know. You have brought joy to my life and made me a better version of myself. Words cannot express how happy I am that we are about to start the next phase of our lives together.....Arthur, it is with your help and influence that I felt the confidence to chase my dream, and for that, I can never thank you enough....Dannie, you make Arthur happier than I have ever seen, you are a truly amazing person, and I am honoured to call you my friend...."

Jane went round the room in turn, showering her guests with love and admiration. As she looked at the smiling faces of her family and friends, Jane noticed she wasn't the only one overcome, eyes glistened like stars with tears of joy. The room buzzed with warmth and electricity that only family can bring.

"I'm sorry, call it pregnancy hormones, but what I'm trying to say is, I love you all so much. I am so grateful that our little one will have such an amazing group of people to help guide and influence him or her. Wow, I guess dreams do come true because I am filled with so much gratitude right now. Everything I have ever wanted and everyone I have ever loved is right here in these walls," Jane smiled, wiping a stray tear from her eye.

Kennedy stood with her wife, hugging her tightly as her guests clapped and cheered, sharing in an embrace.

"Shall we tell them?" Kennedy whispered.

Jane nodded and took Kennedy's hand while holding her bump with the other.

"Ladies and gentlemen, we have an announcement to make," Kennedy said.

"Oh my god, you're pregnant," Lucia joked, making the group howl with laughter.

"We have hinted but are finally ready to reveal our chosen name. Be it a boy or a girl, we would like you all to welcome.... Morgan," Kennedy cheered.

⸱⸱⟩⟩✦⟨⟨⸱⸱

With the main course finished, George and Ben helped clear the table. With everyone fully relaxed, Jane and Kennedy agreed it was time to get the mystery underway. Kennedy slipped her hand under the table and pressed the button on her phone. A bloodcurdling, bone-chilling scream erupted through the house, playing through the many scattered speakers Kennedy had programmed. Mrs Tree jumped, dropping her champagne flute and shattering it on the floor.

"A bit extreme, don't you think, honey?" Jane asked, raising an eyebrow at Kennedy.

"I didn't listen to the track before I loaded it. I found it online," Kennedy shrugged.

Ronald and Mrs Tree hurried to clean up their mess as the guests slowly realised the games had begun. They were eyeing each other with suspicion. Some rechecked their clues before the room erupted in question.

"What was that?"

"Has the game begun?"

"Who screamed?"

"Where did it come from?"

Jane and Kennedy chuckled, watching as their loved ones' competitive sides kicked in and people teamed up to hunt for clues around the house. Following the screams, everyone was reluctant to go into the loft space.

"Well done, ladies. This is going to be fun," Arthur grinned, teaming up with Kennedy's uncle Lucas, a fellow police officer.

Jane sat back, watching her mother scratching her head, trying to figure out the riddle she had found hidden in the pictures on the mantle. Leslie kept a close eye on Rochelle, determined to beat her, as did Rochelle with Leslie. It was proving a great form of entertainment.

"Okay, so our first mystery is deciphering who was killed and where?" Dannie asked.

"Exactly; if all the guests were in the dining room, who could the victim be?" Lucia asked.

"I honestly thought the victim would be one of us," Yvette said.

"Why would I do that? Then one of you would have to sit the game out because you would be dead. This way, everyone can get involved," Jane smiled.

As the guests dispersed around the home, suddenly Rochelle came charging down the stairs waving a clue in hand, excited she had figured out the next step.

"I found this in the attack," she cheered.

"What does it say?" Leslie asked.

Rochelle unfolded the piece of paper and read the clue aloud to all the guests.

"You have looked high; now it's time to look low. Before you know it, my name you will know."

# CHAPTER 4

"You guys don't have a basement, do you?" Ben asked.

"No, Dad. Basements aren't really a feature in UK homes," Kennedy laughed.

As the guests tried to decipher their clues, putting together puzzles and answering riddles, leading them to the next clue, another scream erupted. Unfortunately, while this scream didn't echo through each room in the house, it was just as terrifying.

"What, another victim?" Lucia asked, frustrated as she had just worked out her latest clue.

"No, Kennedy must have pressed the button by mistake," Jane answered.

"No, I didn't. My phone is on charge in the office," Kennedy said, confused, looking to Jane for answers.

Panicked, Jane waddled from room to room, checking that all her loved ones were safe and unharmed, while Kennedy rushed upstairs to check on the budding detectives upstairs. Everyone was present and accounted for, and everyone had heard the scream.

Unsure what was happening, the guests gathered in the dining room, looking at each other to see who had screamed. Was it an effort to throw the others off their game? Was someone closer to winning than Jane and Kennedy would have liked so early on in the game?

"It sounded like it came from outside," Dannie said.

"No one has been in the garden," Jane said.

That fact annoyed Jane; she thought she had made her clues simple enough for even a novice detective to gather that the clues were leading them to the garden shed.

"It might just be next door, kids. They probably heard the scream and wanted to be involved in the game, too," Leslie shrugged.

Kennedy and Arthur's eyes locked; something wasn't quite right.

"Tell you what, let me go have a look outside," Arthur nodded, heading into the garden alone.

⸫⸫⸫⸫

The house grew thick with tension as everyone waited for Arthur to return. Dannie waited anxiously at the window, fiddling with the star and moon pendant hanging around her neck. Leslie and Rochelle were still in game mode, working through their clues and sneaking a peak at others.

"How about we tuck into the dessert while we wait to continue the game? We have plenty to choose from," Jane smiled, heading to the kitchen.

Jane had prepared her famous carrot cake and decorated it with vanilla buttercream. Leslie had brought chocolate brownies and Rochelle, her famous pecan pie. Arthur had brought a Victoria sponge – shop-bought, as he burnt his first and second attempt at baking. Everyone seemed to bring a dessert. As Kennedy and Jane lay the desserts on the table, they realised they had too much. Cakes, pies, cupcakes, cookies, they would have dessert for days.

"I'll make a pot of tea and coffee, too," Kennedy whispered, keeping a close eye on the shed.

Everyone could see Arthur pacing back and forth from the dining room windows in front of the shed. He had his phone in hand, in deep conversation. Dannie tugged harder on her necklace, feeling Arthur's tension even from a distance.

Jane and Kennedy busied themselves, trying to defuse the tension. Finally, Jane convinced Lucia to perform her latest drama monologue from college to entertain the guests. Initially, she was reluctant, but her performance was so captivating that it proved just what the group needed.

⸱⸱⟩⟩ ⟫ ✳ ⟨ ⟨⟨⸱⸱

Arthur snuck back in, careful not to alarm anyone. He pulled Kennedy and Dannie to one side. His face was troubled, and his brow furrowed.

"We need to keep everyone inside. This is now an active crime scene," Arthur whispered.

"What? The dummy in the shed is fake, Arthur. I know how realistic it looked; I jumped myself when I opened the box," Kennedy chuckled, not believing their home could be the scene of a crime.

"The dummy isn't the only body in there," Arthur said.

"Oh, my goodness," Dannie gasped.

"I've called the forensic team and the ME, but until they get here, Dannie, would you mind taking a look and see what you think the cause of death could be?" Arthur asked.

"Of course," Dannie agreed, following Arthur back outside.

Kennedy looked at the party guests as they clapped and cheered at Lucia's performance. Jane was so happy. Kennedy's heart sank that she would have to ruin Jane's evening. Kennedy also worried about what the undue stress would do to Jane and the baby. Sighing, deciding it was better to pull the plaster off in one go, she tapped Jane on the shoulder, pulling her into the kitchen away from the group.

"Don't panic, but someone is dead in the shed," Kennedy blurted out.

"What?" Jane gasped.

"That scream was someone being murdered. Dannie and Arthur are examining the body now, and the ME and a forensic team are on the way. The police will be swarming the house in no time," Kennedy warned.

"What are we going to do? Who is it?" Jane asked, rubbing her baby bump in concern.

"I don't know."

⊶⊱✻⊰⊷

"Do you know this man?" Arthur asked, showing the Daniels a picture of the body in their shed.

"Oh my gosh, that's Mr Wolf from next door," Jane gasped.

"What was he doing in our shed?" Kennedy wondered.

"We can figure that out when the forensic team arrives. But, right now, we need to find out where everyone was at the time of the murder," Arthur ran his hands through his thick greying hair.

Nodding with sombre faces, Jane and Kennedy headed back to their guests. Slowly they explained the situation as best they could.

"Jeez, Jane. When you said murder mystery dinner, I didn't think you would commit so strongly to the performance," Lucia joked.

"This is no joke, I'm afraid. The police will be here any minute," Jane sighed.

The room fell silent. No one believed a word, all waiting and hoping someone would jump up and say it was all part of the game. How could it not be?

"Wait, you're serious?" Ben asked.

Kennedy nodded, and the room fell into an uncomfortable silence.

"So, we are all suspects then, right?" Yvette asked.

Again, Kennedy nodded, and the room took on a new type of tension. Looks of sorrow turned to looks of concern before eventually turning to looks of suspicion. A once harmonious, loving group now all eyed each other in fear. Jane felt her chest grow tight, and she stroked her hand softly over her heart to try and ease her tension.

"Oooh," Jane gasped lightly, clutching her hand to her side.

Baby Morgan was feeling the tension too.

*It's Braxton-hicks, that's all. Morgan isn't due for another week;* Jane convinced herself.

# CHAPTER 5

Once the police and forensic teams arrived, everyone split into separate rooms. Rochelle and Ben headed to the spare room, Leslie and George headed to Jane and Kennedy's room, and the other guests divided between the kitchen, lounge, dining room, and living room. Jane sat on the sofa, rubbing the right side of her belly. The stress of having her loved ones questioned brought on pains that she kept trying to ignore.

When Mrs Tree noticed the neighbours gathering outside their homes looking for gossip on what had happened inside, she took it upon herself to close all the curtains to offer privacy. Yet all it did was cast darkness, matching the atmosphere that unnerved everyone further.

Kennedy bounced between Arthur and the officers and ensured the guests were topped up with tea and coffee. Seconds felt like minutes, minutes felt like hours, as the police questioned each guest in turn, not wanting to let anyone go until they had more answers.

"Jane, you need to rest," Kennedy worried as Jane joined her at the kitchen window.

"I'm going crazy sitting and doing nothing. I need to know what's going on," Jane sighed, rubbing her belly a little more.

"So far, I've been told nothing. Even Arthur has been pushed out as he is technically a suspect too."

"He won't be happy with that," Jane said.

Arthur's partner, Lieutenant Harper, had taken over the investigation. Arthur tried his hardest to get involved but was warned that he would be arrested for obstruction if he didn't stay out of it. Arthur paced the hallway anxiously as Dannie sat on the stairs, watching, playing with her necklace.

᠄ᢀᢀᢀ᠄

By the time the forensic team left, it was early morning hours, and Mr Wolf's body was taken from the scene. Arthur, Jane, Kennedy, and Dannie headed into the garden to speak with Lieutenant Harper.

"Do you know what happened?" Dannie asked when the others were all too nervous to speak.

"It looks like he was stabbed several times. Whomever it was, was angry because these puncture marks are too deep and frantic to be self-defence. But I can also rule out anyone inside as a suspect," Lieutenant Harper said.

"How so?" Arthur asked.

"Skins cells under the deceased fingernails says he fought back. None of your guests had scratches on them. Also, there is a void in the blood on the floor where the killer stands. Finally, none of your guests has blood on their shoes," Harper answered.

"So you are saying Mr Wolf was killed inside the shed? He wasn't dragged there? Who would come into someone else's garden just to kill someone?" Jane panicked.

"I'd say someone who wanted to frame you two for the murder," Dannie said sadly.

"We are just gathering the last bits of evidence, then we will be out of your hair," Harper patted Kennedy on the shoulder.

A team of forensic officers emerged from the shed carrying items splattered with blood, including Jane's life-like dummy from the party.

"Wait, something is missing," Jane yelled, waddling over to the officer holding the dummy.

"Please don't touch, miss."

"Kennedy look, the knife is missing," Jane pointed to the hole in the dummy's chest.

"Knife?" Arthur asked.

"Yeah, the dummy had a knife plunged in its chest. It came like that from the prop store. I never thought it was a real knife. If anything, I thought the hilt was glued on," Jane gasped.

"You don't think that's the murder weapon, do you?" Kennedy asked.

"I'm sure we find the killer when we find the knife. We start interviewing your neighbours tomorrow," Harper said, urging the officers to leave.

⋙⋙✳⋘⋘

With Lieutenant Harper giving the guests the all-clear to leave, Jane and Kennedy bid everyone a good night. Everyone was ordered to hand their passports to the station the following morning. No one was to leave town until the killer had been caught.

"Jane, I'm worried about you. You have been rubbing your stomach all day. Is everything okay? Should we go to the hospital?" Kennedy asked as she helped Jane to bed.

"No, I'm fine. It's Braxton-hicks, you know, false labour. It's probably due to the stress. So don't worry," Jane smiled, but her eyes held concern.

Kennedy knew not to push and decided to stay up all night to tend to Jane. Jane didn't sleep much either that night. The few times Kennedy's eyes had grown too heavy, Jane had slipped out of bed and downstairs. Kennedy found her at the kitchen window, staring out at the shed.

"Baby, come back to bed," Kennedy yawned.

"Why would someone want to frame us?" Jane asked, a lump in her throat.

"Lieutenant Harper will figure that out, sweetie. All you need to worry about now is little Morgan," Kennedy yawned, gently urging Jane back to bed.

No matter what Jane tried, that night's sleep wouldn't come. All she could see whenever she closed her eyes was her long-time neighbour dead in her shed. She had known Mr Wolf for years, and he had always been a pillar of the community. He was the type of man to go out of his way to help, always had a smile and was loved by everyone. Jane wracked her mind to think of a reason someone would want to kill him in such an angry and violent way.

·»))›*‹((«·

By dinner time the following day, Kennedy had tried everything to get Jane to eat, but she had no appetite. Then, still suffering from Braxton-hicks, Jane thought that Kennedy had the right idea. If the pain didn't stop, she would agree to go to the hospital.

A knock on the door offered the distraction Jane needed, and Arthur had returned alone. After being cleared as a suspect, Lieutenant Harper had agreed to allow him to help with the investigation. Arthur had spent all day interviewing the neighbours and had already devised a theory of his own.

"So you think his wife killed him and then took off?" Kennedy asked, handing Arthur a leftover piece of carrot cake.

"That's what it looks like. Mr Wolf's stepdaughter Denise seemed pretty upset. She said her mother and stepfather had been arguing. Denise had gone to her room and put on her headphones stuck in a video game to mask the sounds of yelling. She said she hadn't seen her mother since," Arthur said between bites.

"You don't think that's the entire story, do you?" Jane asked.

Arthur shook his head, taking another bite of cake and a sip of tea. Dabbing his mouth, Jane could practically see the cog turning in his mind as he tried to piece together the mystery.

"We tracked Mrs Wolf's car via CCTV. She was at her mother's house twenty-five miles away at the time of the murder. I think the stepdaughter had something to do with it. She kept pulling at her sleeves, ensuring her arms were covered, and from the witness reports, the scream they heard was female," Arthur stated.

"But what would her motive be?" Kennedy asked.

"That's what we need to figure out."

# CHAPTER 6

The next day at the police station, Lieutenant Harper and Detective Gottfried gathered what evidence they had so far and pinned it to the bulletin board. The centre was a picture of Mr Wolf's body from the shed. Next was a line of suspects – his wife and stepdaughter. They wrote the time of death, the murder weapon and a few other details and stepped back to review it.

"What's that?" Arthur asked, pointing to the CCTV footage of Mrs Wolf's car.

"That's his wife," Harper replied.

Arthur took a step closer, examining the grainy image of a woman wearing sunglasses and a hat. The woman looked much younger than Arthur had thought she would be to have a sixteen-year-old daughter.

"That's not Mrs Wolf," Arthur said, pulling the image down and looking closer.

"It's her car."

"But that's not her driving," Arthur pointed out.

"What's this?" Arthur asked, pointing to another image of Mr Wolf's body.

"It's the crime scene. Arthur, are you feeling, okay?"

"I told you I should have been involved from the get-go," Arthur shook his head.

In the few hours they had been reviewing what Harper had gathered so far, Arthur was already noticing details that should have been glaringly obvious. Shaking his head, Arthur took the image and headed out of the room.

"Where are you going?" Harper yelled after him.

"To the evidence locker and to get a warrant," Arthur replied.

⋙⟫✦⟪⋘

Arthur had done the right thing. His main suspect was about to board a plane to Europe when his team apprehended her. The killer might have gotten away if Arthur had figured it out just a few minutes later.

The evidence was shaky at best, but Arthur knew that once he got a confession, the evidence wouldn't matter. And Arthur knew he had enough evidence to make the suspect shake in her boots.

Staring through the double-sided glass, Arthur watched as Denise paced the room, still pulling her sleeves past her hands. Arthur waited a little longer until she sat down, rocking her chair back and forward before sitting straight and bouncing her leg anxiously.

"Harper, come on, we have work to do," Arthur grunted, leading the way to interrogation room C.

Photographs, a warrant, a gold button, and a name were all Arthur had to go on. They still didn't have the murder weapon, but Arthur knew he had the right person in custody.

⋙⟫✦⟪⋘

"Hello, Miss Wolf," Arthur said, taking a seat.

"My name isn't Wolf. I have my biological father's last name," Denise said, keeping her eyes on her hands.

"Oh, I know," Arthur grinned, watching as Denise's entire demeanour changed.

"You can't interview me alone. I'm a minor. I need a parent or guardian or a lawyer with me," Denise said, suddenly confident.

"Your father is on his way," Arthur said, sitting back and folding his arms.

Arthur began to mirror Denise, leaning back in his chair and rocking it on the back legs. Then, keeping his eyes trained on her, he waited silently.

The clock's ticking and the chairs' creak were the only sounds. The clock sounded louder with every passing second. Even to Arthur, it was maddening, but it seemed to be doing the trick in agitating Denise more.

A knock on the door alerted the detectives to Martin Cox's arrival. Now things could truly begin.

᠈᠈〉᠈᠅᠊᠊᠊

"Thank you for coming, Mr Cox," Lieutenant Harper said, shaking the man's hand.

"Of course, my sweet girl is accused of murder. Where else would I be? Now can we get this nonsense over with? I want to take my daughter home," Martin groaned, sitting close to his daughter.

"Right then. Denise, when did your mother leave?" Arthur asked.

"I don't know. I was playing my video games."

"For an entire eight weeks? Because her passport was logged heading to America eight weeks ago. Last known location was Ohio," Arthur said, pulling the record from the folder in his lap and sliding it across the table.

"Don't say anything, honey," Martin whispered, glaring at Arthur.

"Is this you?" Arthur asked, sliding the picture of Denise driving her mother's car.

"I don't have my licence yet."

"That's not what I asked," Arthur smirked.

"If this is all you have, I'm taking my daughter home now, and I'm putting in a complaint with the police chief," Martin said, standing and grabbing his daughter's arm.

"Sit down, Mr Cox; I will get to you in a second," Arthur snapped, glaring back at Martin until he sat down.

# CHAPTER 7

Days had passed since Mr wolf's murder, and it was time to explain precisely what had happened to the Daniels. As Arthur and Dannie pulled up to Jane and Kennedy's house, the same line of cars sat outside, including the cherry red Jaguar Arthur hadn't been able to stop thinking about.

Knocking on the door, Kennedy answered with a smile, immediately wrapping Dannie and Arthur in a big hug.

"It's so good to see you come in; there is someone I want you to meet," Kennedy led them through to the living room.

Sitting on the sofa, wrapped in a little blue blanket in Leslie's arms, was a beautiful baby boy. Thick dark ringlets of hair sprouted on his head, and large brown eyes blinked at the sea of smiling faces admiring him before he gently slipped back to sleep.

"Arthur, Dannie, meet Morgan," Jane smiled.

Jane was still very tired and was happy to let her relatives enjoy cuddling Morgan or two as the tiny bundle of joy was passed from relative to relative.

"Congratulations. When did you go into labour?" Dannie asked, leaning in to hug Jane.

"The night of the murder. I had been having what I thought was

Braxton-hicks all day. At half four in the morning, my waters finally broke. Kennedy delivered Morgan at home."

"You did?" Arthur gasped.

"Yeah, I called the ambulance, but Jane's labour progressed really quickly. So with the help of the nine-nine-nine operator, I delivered Morgan," Kennedy beamed with pride, joining Jane on the sofa and wrapping an arm around her shoulder.

"Wait, if Dannie and Arthur didn't know that you had given birth, they didn't come round to see the baby. Why are they here?" Lucia asked.

"Lucia, don't be rude," Leslie snapped.

"It's fine. You are quite the detective, Lucia. In fact, it's a good thing everyone is here. We have solved Mr Wolf's murder," Arthur said.

⊸⊱⊰✳⊱⊰⊷

Getting everyone a cup of tea and a slice of cake and finding Dannie and Arthur a chair, George and the others sat waiting anxiously for every detail of the case.

"It was his wife, wasn't it?" shot one voice.

"Why was he killed in the shed?"

"Who killed him?" came another voice.

"What was the motive?"

Settling everyone down, Arthur sipped his tea, waiting for the room to quiet.

"One question at a time, please," Arthur grinned, secretly loving all eyes on him.

"How did you figure it out?" Kennedy asked, taking hold of her son.

Arthur proceeded to explain how when he had interviewed the neighbours, Denise's demeanour had piqued his interest. She insisted on keeping her arms covered, and her jacket was missing a button. When Arthur was allowed to join the case, he noticed a gold button in the crime scene photos, covered in Mr Wolf's blood. When he saw that the CCTV of Mrs Wolf showed a much younger woman, he completed a search for her passport and credit cards and found she had left for America eight weeks before. He continued to say that he had checked Denise's gaming ID and found she hadn't logged on for three days before the murder, a detail that blew apart her alibi.

"Wait, Denise killed him? But she is a child," Jane gasped.

"She didn't do it alone," Dannie said.

"Then who did?" Rochelle asked eagerly for another hold of Morgan.

"Her father. Martin Cox."

᠅᠉᠉⟫᠅⟫᠅⟨᠅⟨⟨᠅

"Why?" George asked.

George explained how Mrs Wolf had left weeks prior and as Denise and Mr Wolf had already had a shaky relationship, he never supported her 'gaming career', calling it a pipe dream and a non-starter. However, a week before his murder, Denise was scheduled to travel to Southampton for a gaming competition where the grand prize was a contract with Supersonic Gaming and one hundred thousand pounds.

"When I finally presented her with all the evidence I had, which at this point was very little and circumstantial at best, she cracked. She broke into tears and said that Mr Wolf had torn up her tickets and taken away her games console…."

"Wow, you rest a lot on a bluff, Arthur," Kennedy said.

"Thankfully, it worked," Arthur replied.

"So, she killed him over a game console?" Ben gasped in disgust.

"Not just the console. I looked into her supposed career. For a sixteen-year-old kid, she was pulling in six figures a year. It was just a game to her stepfather, but she had made a lot of money streaming and creating manuals for amateur gamers. After that, she got in touch with her father, asking if she could go live with him, but Mr wolf refused," Arthur stopped to take a sip of tea.

"So, she killed him because of that? What did her father have to do with it? Is he the one who put the body in the shed?" Lucia asked, hooked on the story like it was a soap opera.

"Turns out her rival won the competition she was due to enter. A gamer of much less skill than her," Dannie said, taking hold of Morgan and swaddling him close.

"So, if she had entered, chances are she would have won the contract and the prize money," Jane said.

"Exactly," Arthur nodded.

·»»›❂✳❂‹«««·

Arthur continued to tell the group how Denise had cracked in interrogation, screaming with rage until her father jumped in to protect her.

"I saw the two women from next door put a Halloween prop in the shed, so I thought if I could get Andrew in there, it would look like they killed him, not me," Denise had cried.

"He took me away from my dad and drove my mother away, then tried to destroy my career. Do you know what my life would be like if I had won that contract? And I would have won, you know!" Denise screamed.

"I told him I needed help with the lawn mower they said I could borrow, and when he entered the shed with me, I grabbed the shovel and hit him with it. When he went down, I called my dad to come and get me." Denise had sobbed.

Arthur sat back, arms folded, letting the two incriminate each other, making his job that much easier.

"When I arrived, I heard her scream and ran into the garden next door. Her hand was bleeding. That creep had attacked her, and she had fought back. So, it was self-defence," Martin insisted.

"It's funny you should say that because I have a warrant here to examine Denise's arms and to take a sample of her skin cells," Lieutenant Harper chimed in, tossing the warrant from his pocket on the table.

"I think Denise is telling the truth, but I also think that before you arrived, Mr Cox that Mr Wolf woke up and fought back. I think it began as self-defence on his part, and Denise stabbed him. Then, when you arrived, you saw the man trying to keep your daughter away from you and stabbed him five more times," Arthur said.

"I want my lawyer," Martin Cox demanded.

·››·›✳·‹·‹‹·

"I told you that stupid dummy was excessive," Kennedy mocked.

"Noted. No more murder mystery dinners," Jane laughed.

"What else? What else?" Lucia cheered, earning a round of shushes from the group as she almost woke Morgan.

"I was right, of course. When Mr Wolf woke up, he tried to escape, but Denise had pulled the knife. He scratched her arm, and when she stabbed him, she sliced her hand. When Mr Cox arrived, he finished the job, leaving Mr Wolf in the shed. When we came out to investigate, they hurried back around the bushes into their garden, and Denise dressed as he mother and took her car. A few miles between her and her grandmother's house, Denise disposed of the murder weapon. We retrieved it this morning. It's quite clever, really. She thought if she was seen on CCTV dressed as her mother and the murder weapon was found, it would implicate Mrs Wolf for the murder," Arthur continued.

"Why frame her mother?" Dannie asked.

"She was hurt that her mother had ripped her from her father and abandoned her when her marriage fell apart. She is a furious kid who needs help."

·››·›✳·‹·‹‹·

As the weeks passed since Mr Wolf's murder, news of the famous gamer who killed her stepfather spread like wildfire. But, with both Denise and Martin confessing, the trial was short. Martin was sentenced to twenty years for first-degree murder. And since Denise was still a minor, she could only be sentenced to two years in juvenile detention before becoming an adult and being released.

"That doesn't seem fair. She practically got away with it," Jane complained.

"Unfortunately, that's the way the law works. We can't re-try her as an adult once she turns eighteen. Juvenile detention can only hold her until she is legally an adult," Arthur sighed.

Even with a killer behind bars, the victory was bittersweet. Justice didn't feel like it had been done.

"Please tell me she isn't moving back here when she gets out?" Jane panicked, clutching baby Morgan closer to her.

"No, Mr Wolf's oldest son is selling the house. I don't know what will happen to Denise when she gets out. Unless his mother returns from the States, she has no one else. Her father was her only relative."

"What about her grandmother?" Kennedy asked.

"She wants nothing to do with her," Dannie finished.

"It's heartbreaking. A man is dead, and a kid's life is ruined because of a moment's anger. My heart goes out to Mr Wolf's son. How awful must it feel knowing your father's killer will be set free in two years?" Jane sighed.

"Technically, Mr Cox killed him. He was still alive when he arrived. So the most Denise could be charged with was ABH."

⋙❉⋘

As the weeks passed and all the drama surrounding Mr Wolf's murder subsided, Jane and Kennedy settled into family life. Jane would find herself watching her son sleep for hours, just watching him breathe.

Kennedy had rigged the nursery with all the latest tech. She had set up a starlight projector that showed the night sky above the house reflected on the nursery ceiling. A state-of-the-art baby monitoring system while they slept alerted them to changes in Morgan's breathing and temperature and allowed them to keep an eye on him from anywhere in the house. Leslie and George suddenly found any excuse to come to visit. And Kennedy's parents had even been thinking about moving to the UK to be closer to their new grandson.

"Hey Mom, no, don't worry, Morgan is sleeping. Hold on, I'll put you on loudspeaker so Jane can hear," Kennedy poked the button and set the phone on the kitchen island.

"Rochelle, Ben, it's so good to hear from you. We miss you already," Jane chimed as she busied herself making lunch.

"Well, you won't have to miss us for much longer," Ben practically sang down the phone.

"Are you coming for another visit?" Kennedy asked.

"Nope. We have bought the house next door; we are moving to England," they cheered down the phone.

When the phone call ended, Kennedy and Jane burst out laughing.

"I know your mother has wanted to move here for years. I just never thought she could convince your dad to do it," Jane laughed.

"She didn't; Morgan did," Kennedy beamed.

A little boy. A ray of light. Morgan was a dream come true, completing the Daniels family and filling the house with even more love. He not only filled a hole in Jane's heart but also brought the entire family closer together. Once divided by an ocean, they would now be right next door.

"How about we have a murder mystery celebration for Morgan's first birthday?" Jane chirped, almost making Kennedy choke on her orange juice.

"I think we have had enough murders around us to last a lifetime. All I want to do now is enjoy being a mom and a wife," Kennedy smiled.

A soft cry emitted through the speakers on the kitchen counter.

"Morgan is awake," Jane grinned.

"Allow me."

**The End.**

# EQUINOX ENIGMA
## A MYSTIC MOONHAVEN MYSTERY

# CHAPTER 1
# EQUINOX AWAKENING

My breath puffed out in a cloud of fog, making me wrinkle my nose. I had hoped this strange cold front would lift once we got out of February, but it was hanging on. It shouldn't be this cold this time of year.

"You okay, Harper?" my walking companion asked.

Detective Liam Ashford and I had gotten into the habit of taking early morning walks before he had to go to the police station and I had to open my bookshop. Normally, we had quite a lively conversation about everything from a TV show we were both watching to whatever newest gossip my friend Ella had to share about our small town, Moonhaven.

"I'm sorry I've been quiet today," I apologized to Liam. "It's the weather. I'm so tired of winter. I know I've only been in Moonhaven for a little over a year, but I don't remember March last year being so cold and snowy still."

"That's because it's usually not," Liam answered. "Moonhaven is usually very mild, especially for this part of the country."

I hummed, shoving my hands into my pockets as a chilly breeze ruffled my hair. "It's going to be the spring equinox in a few days."

Liam snorted and gave me an amused look. "You're not going to say that the equinox has some sort of mystical effect on whether it snows, are you?"

I rolled my eyes at him. The spring equinox was a powerful time for magic, not that Liam would believe it. His feet were firmly planted on the ground, to the point of coming up with perfectly rational explanations for the irrational things that happened around Moonhaven. He had a hard enough time not commenting on the various occult books and crystals I sell at my bookstore.

Sometimes I wondered what his reaction would be if I told him I was a witch. Not that I would—secrecy was the number one rule in these things. So even though I was certain I could summon my flames or winds right in front of him and he still wouldn't believe me, I would not risk it.

"If you think about it, the equinox has the power to stop it from snowing. Seeing as how spring ends the winter," I teased him.

There seemed to be something off this year, though. It had started way back at the beginning of the year when Percival Whitman used ancestral magic to attack the town. The underlying magical disturbance that it caused had lingered ever since and was getting stronger the closer we got to the equinox.

"Ha ha," Liam said, bumping me with his shoulder. "Hilarious."

I stuck my tongue out at him. By this time, we had reached the Bed & Breakfast where I'd ended up as my temporary permanent residence.

Moonhaven didn't have much of a real estate market, and finding an affordable place to live so far had been impossible. I owned my little bookstore outright, though, and was currently trying to figure out if I could build a second floor so I could live where I worked.

The owner of the B&B, Abigail Thorne, was in the living room, shaking her head as she flipped through a book of folk remedies when Liam and I came in.

"Don't bother thinking about a shower," she said, sounding frazzled. "The town just put out a notice. The pipes have frozen up, so there's no running water. They're seeing if they can ship in some bottled water from other towns while they try to fix the problem."

I unwound the scarf from my neck, frowning. "How could they freeze? They're under the ground."

"Don't ask me how." Abigail sighed. "I'm trying to find something that will help poor Ella. That cold of hers is just not going away."

"She should see a doctor," Liam said. He didn't take off his winter gear. "No water, huh? That makes it even worse. I hope we don't make the news. This kind of thing attracts weirdos and do-gooders, and I'm too cold to deal with the logistics."

He looked so disgruntled that I laughed. He hadn't worn a knitted hat today, so his dark hair was ruffled by the wind. With his flannel coat and barely there five o'clock shadow, he looked more like a lumberjack than a police detective. Once he shaved and put on his uniform, though, all ruggedness would disappear.

I had to admit, even though I was more of a firefighter or Coast Guard gal, something about Liam Ashford in his uniform made me confront an unfortunate truth: the man was the most attractive person in all of Moonhaven. And I liked to look at him almost as much as I enjoyed our banter.

"Sounds like you have something else going on," Abigail noted, closing the book of remedies for now. She kept her finger between the pages to mark her spot.

Liam shrugged, then sighed. "I might as well tell you. It'll be all over town soon enough. Someone keeps breaking into the museum. They've taken a few little, inconsequential things, but I can't figure out how or who it is."

"Didn't David Blackwood install security cameras?" I asked, frowning. David was the museum curator.

"That's the frustrating thing. He did. The tapes are all missing, though, and when we checked the cloud, there's nothing. The cover-up seems far too high-tech for what they're taking," Liam explained. "Max Harrington is taking an unnatural interest in it all and, if I had a suspect, it'd be him."

I considered his words. I knew little about Max Harrington, other than he was an old friend of Ella's. But Ella had so many friends in Moonhaven, that didn't give me much to go on.

"Why do you say 'if' you had a suspect, if you suspect Max?"

Abigail asked. Her crinkled eyes were cunning as she picked up on what I'd missed.

Liam grimaced. "I have no proof connecting him. No motive. Nothing. They might as well be disappearing into the ether for what I've been able to find out."

A shiver ran down my spine. "Could it be connected to the Winter Festival?" Percival Whitman tried to steal the documents that proved his family stole the Blackwood land when the town was first founded.

"No. What use would he have for a handkerchief and a teacup? Whitman is in jail for his crimes and there's no reason for him to be attacking the museum."

"Unless he wanted to set up David for something in vengeance," I pointed out.

Then there was what Liam didn't know. Percival had called on an ancient magic in his attacks. A magic that had a lingering disturbance in town. The land issue was still being disputed by both the Blackwoods and the Whitmans. For now, it was in a town trust. The museum had been at the heart of the previous attacks.

It could be at the heart of this disturbance as well.

"Hey." Liam gently took my hand and squeezed. "My guess is that this is all going to blow over. Someone thinks they're being funny. I'm sure nothing will come of it."

I forced a smile in return, not at all confident.

Liam gave my hand one last reassuring squeeze and then turned to go. "I'll call you later."

"Come over for dinner," Abigail offered. "I'm making Shepherd's Pie."

"I'll see if I can make it," Liam promised. He touched his forehead as though tipping his hat. "Ladies."

He opened the door. A burst of fresh cold brought with it the bite of frost. I shivered, my arms wrapped around myself. How did it get colder outside in the few minutes that we were in here?

Abigail hummed as she tapped her chin. "Every thief has a story. Seek the heart, and you'll find more than stolen relics."

Heat blossomed in my cheeks. "Wh-what?"

"Nothing, dear. Come with me. I have something to show you in the greenhouse." Abigail smiled brightly, knowingly, and led me through the B&B.

My face remained hot as I followed. Was Abigail talking about my relationship with Liam? Yes, we'd grown closer over these last few months… At least, I no longer held his pragmatism against him, and he tolerated my wild flights of fancy. Was Abigail telling me to join the case so I could spend more time with him?

Come to think about it, that might not be such a bad idea.

Abigail's greenhouse was connected to the house, and an addition of glass was built onto the south side. Thanks to the space heaters she'd put out here, it was warm and toasty. The sun beamed through the windows, making it feel like spring ought to. The rows on rows of planters we had worked on over the last few months were burgeoning with life.

"Oh, it's beautiful," I exclaimed, clapping my hands lightly.

"Isn't it?" Abigail checked the soil of her row of daffodils. "Even the winter can't hold out forever. New life is blossoming, even if we can't see it everywhere. Feel free to come out here whenever you need to, Harper. I know the constant snow and cold weighs on one's soul."

"Thank you."

I settled into a wicker chair, enjoying the scent of warm soil and plants. As I sat there, surrounded by the growing plants, I felt lighter than I had during my walk with Liam. I hadn't even realized how much of a weight the snow was having on me.

Sitting here, it became all the clearer that something wrong was happening. Whether Percival was behind bars, I knew this was connected to the strange things happening in the museum. Which meant I needed to investigate.

Liam was a brilliant detective, but he was in over his head if magic was involved.

I pulled out my phone and sent him a text.

I want in on this case with you.

It took a few minutes for him to reply.

> There's barely a case. I can handle it.

> Never said you couldn't. But we said we
> wanted to work on a case together that hadn't
> escalated to death or disappearances, right?

I held my breath, waiting. When he didn't answer, I sent another text.

> This would be perfect since you said it was
> probably nothing big. We could make it an
> official work-together case.

> Come to the police station at ten. I'll get the
> paperwork done to make you an official
> consultant.

I sent a thumbs up and slid my phone back into my pocket, grinning. There. That was the first step in figuring out what was going on. Now for the hard part.

# CHAPTER 2
## LOST LEGACY

Ella's Wheel was the most popular coffee shop in Moonhaven. Ella ran the place, and everyone was always eager to see her bright disposition when they showed up. It had been closed for the past week because of Ella's head cold. When I contacted David Blackwood to talk with him about the museum case, he insisted that our meeting happen at the shop.

Ella had, apparently, already agreed. She lived over the shop, so it was easy enough for her to run down and open it up.

"Are you sure?" I asked her as I made coffee with the shiny machine behind the brew bar.

She sat in a booth, nose red and honey-brown hair piled on her head. But she smiled at me. "Oh, I'm more than sure. I've been so bored! I don't even feel that sick. I just don't want to spread my germs all over town."

The door opened, and David Blackwood stepped in. He was a man of medium height and had an academic air. He smiled politely, but he seemed nervous when he looked at me.

"David, take a seat," I told him. "Ella said you asked her to be here, too?"

"If it's alright," he said, sliding into the booth opposite her as she hastily put on a cloth mask and used hand sanitizer on her hands. She took the whole not spreading germs thing seriously.

"It's fine," I assured him. "I am here as an official consultant with the police, but I asked Liam, and he said it was fine. I'll have to record our conversation, though."

David nodded stiffly.

"You want anything?" I asked as I set my finished coffee on the brew bar.

"Decaf, one milk, and sugar," Ella said behind her mask.

David visibly relaxed as he nodded.

As I brewed up the cup for him, a knock came on the door. I turned, and my eyes widened. Max Harrington, Liam's closest thing to a suspect, stood on the other side of the door. Ella scooted out of the booth and answered it.

"I picked you up some cough drops," Max told her. He glanced at David and me but didn't comment. "I hope you feel better."

"Thanks," Ella told me.

Max smiled. "If you need anything—"

"I know. I could use some of your famous Italian wedding soup later."

"I'll bring some around," he promised.

He left, and Ella popped one of the cough drops into her mouth before she sanitized her hands again and returned to the booth. By then, I'd finished the coffee and brought it over. I gave David his decaf and sat next to Ella. I put my phone on record and put it on the table between us.

"This is Harper Nightshade talking with Ella Grace and David Blackwood," I said. "Detective Liam Ashford asked me to talk to you, David, to see if I could offer any insights into what's happening at the museum. Would you like to tell me about the artifacts that were stolen?"

David fidgeted as he stared at the cup in his hands. "A handkerchief that belonged to William Blackwood. A teacup belonging to Charles Whitman. A kettle that belonged to Herbert Sinclair. A plow that belonged to Laurence Mercer, and a sad iron that belonged to the Harrington family."

"A sad iron?" Ella asked.

David turned to her. "Those old irons made from solid iron, heated on the fire, and then used to press clothes. They're called sad irons."

I tapped my chin, thinking. "Those were the five families that founded Moonhaven, weren't they?"

David nodded. "Outside of the town, they have very little worth, though. I can't imagine why anyone would steal them. It's not like you could get anything on the black market for any of it."

On the other hand, it was potentially worth a lot in magic if this was connected to the ancestral magic that Percival used back in January. I'd need to know more about these five founding families.

Abigail had said to seek the heart. Now, she might have been talking about Liam, but she always seemed to know more about what was happening in Moonhaven than she let on. Plus, she'd lived here her whole life, and if anyone would know the town's secret history, it was her.

"This might sound strange, but were there any love affairs between the families?" I asked David. "We know that the Blackwood lands were stolen because Howard Whitman claimed he was married to Penelope Blackwood when he wasn't. Someone might try to use these artifacts to prove something."

"Like what?" Ella asked.

I laughed self-consciously and shrugged. "I'm not sure. But it's worth thinking about, right?"

David looked less than certain, but Ella swallowed my lie. Her eyes sparkled as she leaned forward across the table. "It's a great story, anyway. So. Any sordid love affairs?"

"I'm not sure sordid is the right word," David replied. "But while I was reading her journals, I realized that Penelope Blackwood was in love with Herbert Sinclair. There are no records anything came from it, though."

I leaned back, disappointed. "What about the other families?"

"There were marriages for sure. But nothing particularly scandalous."

Ella hummed as she popped another cough drop into her mouth. "You know what? I've been looking into my family history, and my mother was a descendant of Herbert Sinclair and my father was a descendant of Charles Whitman. If you think about it, Moonhaven's history is four hundred years old. I bet there were a lot of intermarriages between the families since then."

That was a fair point. Just because someone didn't have the same last name as the founding families didn't mean they couldn't have inherited their magic books.

I sighed, resting my chin in my hand. This really didn't get me anywhere closer to where I needed to be. "I doubt that it's someone who thinks that because they're descended from the founders, it means they should have their belongings."

Ella frowned. "You wouldn't think so, but maybe there is. People can be weird sometimes. When I researched my family tree, I went to the cemetery to double-check the dates on the documents I'd found and Percival Whitman just about blew his top when he saw me in the Whitman family section."

David winced at the mention of the man who had attacked him.

"But then we all know that he's not exactly stable," Ella said quickly. She blushed.

"It's fine," David told her. "I don't mind."

I, however, was piqued by this turn of events. "You were researching your family history even before the Winter Festival? You've never brought it up before."

Ella shrugged. "I guess I never thought about it with you. We have so many other things we're talking about. I've been working with Max a lot. Hey, actually, did you know David and I are distant cousins? It's all very amusing."

I smiled at her, but I had a funny feeling sink into my stomach. It seemed strange that she would work with Max Harrington to look into her family tree and not bring anything up.

She sneezed, covering her masked face with both hands, then grabbed the sanitizer.

"Why don't you go wash your hands instead of using more of that stuff?" I suggested, moving out of the booth. "Your skin will dry up, and your hands will crack."

"I really should get back to the museum anyway," David said.

"Do you mind if I come along with you? I'd like to look around," I blurted. Ella was looking tired, her cheeks pink with a fever.

I almost took back my question so I could take Ella to the hospital, but she caught my eye and frowned. "Don't go worrying over me, Harper. That's what everyone's doing. Abigail's going to be over here before you know it. I'm fine. You go on with David."

David hadn't actually agreed to take me to the museum. The disgruntled expression on his face told me he would rather I didn't go. But Ella was looking so miserable he apparently didn't want to say no in front of her.

We took our coffee to-go, and I made Ella promise to text me if she got worse. Then David and I headed toward the museum in his car. I'd call Liam to come pick me up so I could fill him in with what little I'd found out.

The drive was tense, but as we drew closer to the museum, David broke the silence.

"When I was in a coma in January, I kept seeing your face in my dreams," he said.

I bit my lips together. It wasn't surprising. His spirit kept coming to me while he was in his coma, giving me clues to find him.

"I'm sorry that I'm so on edge around you," he continued, his voice softening. "I don't mean to, but I still associate you with everything that happened."

"That's not your fault. I'm sorry that I'm making it worse for you."

David sighed. "But you saved me. I remember that much."

Something about the way he said it made goosebumps break out over my skin. Did he remember the magic that had taken him out into the woods in the first place? The frost wolfs that had dragged him away and nearly killed him?

I swallowed as I looked out the window. "I did what I could. It was all so frightening I barely remember anything."

"I've always wondered who the anonymous person who told Detective Ashford where to find me was," he prodded.

"Me, too," I said. I didn't have to act with that one. It was a complete mystery to me as well.

We arrived at the museum, only to find the front door wide open.

David groaned. "Great. It's happened again."

I took off my seatbelt nervously. "They won't be in there waiting for us, will they?"

"No. They're always gone. Besides, there's a back door. We just have to make a lot of noise," David assured me.

If he was calm about it, I saw no reason to be alarmed myself. I called Liam, and we headed inside.

"If you're still here, you'd better scram," David yelled. "We already called the police. I—"

He paused just inside the doorstop.

I ran into him and bounced off. "Sorry—"

Then I saw why he'd stopped. The glass case that stood in the middle of the welcome room was empty. My eyes widened as I scrambled to remember what was there... the bell. The big bronze bell that had to weigh half a ton was missing.

"How?" David breathed. "That bell has been part of Moonhaven since its founding. Why would anyone take it?"

# CHAPTER 3
## BLOOMING SECRETS

Liam arrived at the museum shortly. His anxious expression melted into relief once he saw both David and me sitting in the welcoming area. He strode over to us, only to falter when he noticed the empty display case.

"What happened?" he asked, his eyes widening.

"Someone stole the bell," David replied glumly.

I rubbed my arms as Liam ran a hand through his hair. "None of the alarms were tripped. What about the footage?"

David shook his head. "Same as before. Nothing. I guess we know what the thief was doing. They must have been testing the systems to see if they could pull it off. I don't get it."

"Is it valuable?" I asked. Until now, he'd been so lost in his own thoughts, I didn't want to ask.

"It's not worth much. Not in terms of pure materials or even for collectors. Bells like that aren't all that rare." David stood and paced to the display case. "It's not even the most valuable artifact in the museum."

Liam pulled out a little notebook and jotted down a few notes. "Was anything else taken this time?"

David shook his head. "Not that I've seen. I haven't taken a thorough look at the archives yet, though."

"Once you've completed that, get back to me," Liam said. His brow furrowed. "It seems this is bigger than we previously thought."

I stood. "David, do you have any books about the founding families? Everything that the thief has taken has been connected to something related to the founding of Moonhaven. Maybe there's something in history that will give us a motive."

David and Liam both looked skeptical, but when I met Liam's gaze, he nodded. I gave him a small smile in return. He might not understand everything I was doing, but he would let me take this in the direction I thought might lead somewhere. I was grateful for that.

"These books here are related to the founders," David said, pointing at a shelf of red-bound books. "The sign-out sheet is on my desk. I'll get it."

As he went to the desk, Liam shifted closer to me. "Want to share your hunch?"

"I think this might be another Percival situation. I just want to know if there's a reason for any of the families still in town to take any of these things. Trying to stake their claim or something," I whispered back.

Liam frowned at me. He searched my face, and I stared back, wondering what he was looking for.

Did he suspect that there was more than what I was letting on? He broke away before I could figure it out. I was left distinctly unsettled as David handed me the sign-out sheet. I wrote my name on them, then paused. Max Harrington had signed out each of the books several times since January. Coincidence?

He had seen David at the coffee shop earlier. He'd know that it was empty.

Once I had the books, Liam drove me back to the B&B. I told him about Max signing out the books and he nodded once, but said nothing in response.

Back at the B&B, I called up Ella. "Hey, you want to come to the inn and help me read through a bunch of dry history books?"

Ella laughed, sounding wheezy. "Yes, please. I'm bored out of my head."

I took the most promising book to the front room, where I sat reading and watching for Ella. She arrived shortly, dropped off by Max Harrington. I frowned. First, he showed up at the coffee shop and now this... did he suspect I was onto him?

Onto him how, though? I had only the vaguest suspicions about him and wouldn't even suspect him if Liam didn't.

"Oh, good," Abigail said when Ella came in. "I was just going to make myself a bit of tea. I'll whip something up to help you with that cold of yours."

Ella's eyes pinched into a smile, though her mouth was hidden by a mask. "That sounds wonderful. Thank you."

"I figure we can go out to the greenhouse to read there," I told her, clutching the book to my chest. "It'll be more pleasant in the fresh life of all those growing plants."

Ella glanced outside, where a fresh skiff of snow had dusted everything, and nodded fervently. We got set up, Abigail joining us. We each had a book and read in silence as we sipped at our tea. Mine felt warm and cozy, making me invigorated. I'd have to ask for the recipe—this was much better for concentration than coffee was.

"There were an awful lot of feuds between the five founding families," Ella said after some time. She had stopped coughing and looked much more relaxed and healthier. "It looks like the Sinclairs and the Blackwoods had a genuine friendship between the two. The Sinclairs helped the Blackwoods after they lost their lands to the Whitmans."

"And the Harringtons were linked with the Whitmans through marriage," I said, tracing my finger over the wedding registries I'd come across. "It seems like the Harringtons were always closely allied to them. It was the Harringtons that claimed to be witnesses to Howard Whitman marrying Penelope Blackwood."

Abigail sighed as she closed her book. "And there are so many accusations of theft and land disputes. It's a miracle that Moonhaven didn't tear itself apart."

She looked distinctly unsettled, but before I could ask for more about it, Ella shut her book with a snap. "I guess I should have read through these books while looking for my family history. As it turns out, I'm a direct descendant of all five of the original founders."

"Are you?" Abigail asked. Her brow furrowed.

"Looks like it. I—" Ella sneezed.

The hair on the back of my neck rose as a magical sensation swooshed through the air. The lights blinked off, and the space heater ground to a stop. My eyes widened even as the lingering heat of the greenhouse battled against the cold seeping through the glass windows.

Oh, no. Ella looked up at the lights with a bewildered expression. But I was putting together the dates. Moonhaven was getting warmer again... until Ella got sick. I'd originally thought she got sick because of the cold, but what if it was the other way around? Every time her fever spiked, we got a new snowfall.

Now she sneezed, and the power went out. Coincidence? Not with that magic I felt in the air with her.

"I'll go start a fire in the old wood stove," Abigail said, standing.

"Thanks," Ella croaked. She looked suddenly miserable, though moments ago she'd been healthy enough. She sipped her tea and spat it back out. "It's gone cold."

I stood and set my book aside. "Let's get inside. Don't want you getting colder than you already are."

Ella nodded, pulling her mask on again. She seemed weak now, so I helped her into the living room where Abigail worked on starting a fire. I bundled Ella into blankets, and while Abigail's back was turned to me, I whispered a spell and sent my seeking winds out around Ella.

"Ooh, there's a draft," she said, shivering.

The winds returned to me, relaying back what they had sensed. It made my stomach drop. Ella was in the crosshairs of a powerful, very complex spell. I couldn't get a closer read on it, but I knew it was bad.

Someone was stealing items that belonged to the founders of Moonhaven, and Ella was caught in a powerful spell that was freezing the town. That couldn't be a coincidence, either, which meant it was connected.

Connected to the events with Percival Whitman during the Winter Festival, too. History had shown the Harringtons were the Whitmans' stooges and Max Harrington was showing a peculiar interest in Ella. But why? What was he hoping to do? What was he going to get out of it all?

And, more importantly, was he a witch? Percival had an ancestral magic that he used to summon those frost-wolves. Is Max also using magic, or is this spell on Ella a latent spell in Moonhaven that was triggered by Percival's actions? With the amount of feuds in the founding families, they could have cursed each other.

Ella was descended from them all. But I couldn't believe it was just a coincidence that she alone was affected by this. She couldn't be the only one in town descended from all five founders.

No, this felt deliberate.

I needed more information. I needed to find out exactly what was going on here. I needed to find Max Harrington and see exactly how much he knew. I needed to find the artifacts he stole and find out what spells he was using them for.

Abigail made Ella a fresh cup of tea. As she drank, the lights flickered back on. I sank into a chair, rubbing my temples.

"I should go home and sleep," Ella groaned. "I feel awful."

"No, you'll stay right here," Abigail said firmly. "I don't have any guests right now, so I'll make up a room for you. Just sit there and relax. Harper can lend you some pajamas. The two of you are practically the same size."

"I'll help you," I volunteered.

Abigail nodded. As we were making up the room, I saw the worry heavy on Abigail's face, too. I wished I could explain to her everything that was going on. But I couldn't share my magic with anyone, even though Abigail had almost found out about it during the Winter Festival. If she hadn't hit her head, she'd know everything right now.

"Do you have any clues of who's behind the thefts?" Abigail asked me.

I shook my head. "I think it must have to do with the history of Moonhaven, but I don't know what to do."

"You should start where the first building in Moonhaven was constructed. Oh, it's just an empty spot of land now, but Ella knows where it is. She'll be well enough in the morning to take you out there," Abigail said, sounding distracted.

"I don't think it's a good idea to take Ella out anywhere in her condition."

Abigail shook her head. "Nonsense. Getting fresh air will be good for her. Besides, I'm sure once the equinox passes, this strange cold snap will disappear."

The equinox. It was only two days away. A chill washed over me as I realized what this meant. The Spring Equinox was a powerful time for magic. If I couldn't undo the spell on Ella by them, it might be too late.

I had to have Ella with me, so I could counter the spell as soon as I figured out how and why it was placed.

Otherwise, Moonhaven might lose her forever.

# CHAPTER 4
## ANCESTRAL WHISPERS

The next morning, I woke up to good news and bad news. The good news—Ella was feeling much better. She had a spring to her step and the occasional sniffle was the only sign she was still sick. The bad news —the power lines all throughout Moonhaven had gone dead.

There was no apparent reason for it, no damage that anyone could find. People grumbled about it, but to me it was clear what was happening. Magic. Whatever spell was being used was growing more powerful as we got closer to the equinox. I hoped that Ella feeling better meant she was resistant to the magic, but I didn't have much time to figure it all out.

"Ella and I are going to the site where the first building in Moonhaven was built," I told Liam during our morning walk. The air was bitterly cold, and I wished I'd brought a scarf with me.

The cellphone towers were still working, thank goodness. But who knew how long that would last?

"What do you hope to find there?" he asked me.

"I'm not sure," I admitted, turtling into my coat. "But if the thief is obsessed with Moonhaven history, maybe they've been there, too?"

Liam nodded. "Sound thinking. Just be careful."

"Have you found any more evidence indicating Max Harrington is part of this?" I asked him.

"Yesterday, he stopped by the museum and told David he shouldn't be so worried about the break-ins. I'm not sure if that's suspicious or just socially unaware," Liam said, shaking his head. The wind picked up, bringing with it a bite of frost. "You and Ella be careful out there today."

"We will," I promised.

∞))◆✳❀((∞

The spot where the first building of Moonhaven had been erected was several miles out of town. It had been built by Herbert Sinclair; later, when the Whitmans took control politically and financially, they moved the town lines to where it was today. Everything was written out on a plaque in front of the raised stone edges where the foundation had once been.

"It's strange that there's not more snow around here," Ella said as she stood in the middle of where the building had once been. "Look, there's even fresh grass here."

I crouched, touching the ground. Within the foundation of the building, it was clear of snow and growing green. Strange. I glanced at Ella; her back was to me, so I turned my hand over and whispered a spell for my scouting winds. They spread out around me, rustling over the fresh grass—

I sensed the trap just before it sprung. I shouted and lunged for Ella, but as soon as I grabbed her, a rush of magic sprang up from the ground. Bright lights blinded me. Ella cried out, clutching at me.

Then everything was dark. My heart echoed in my ears as I gasped for breath. I still held onto Ella. We both trembled.

"What was that?" she whispered. "I think I've gone blind."

Her words echoed strangely. The chilly air was warmer, much warmer, and as I pulled in a deep breath to calm myself, I caught the scent of... minerals? Damp soil? I fumbled in my pocket and pulled out my cell phone. The screen lit up, illuminating the surrounding area.

Ella's face glowed in the light from the phone. She looked around and her jaw dropped. "Are we in a cave?"

I went to open the flashlight of my phone only for my stomach to drop. With the power outage, it hadn't charged. I only had about five percent left. I needed to save the power to call for help when we got out of here.

I turned it off, and Ella whimpered. "We need light."

"I know." I reached for her hand and squeezed it.

It wouldn't do us any good to stay in here, lost in the darkness. But I had to conserve the power. Which meant I only had one choice left. My stomach quivered as I took a deep breath.

"Ella?"

"Harper?"

"I'm going to do something... and I need you to stay calm, okay?"

Ella's hands tightened around my arm. "Don't leave me!"

In response, I held my hand out palm-up. I summoned my flames and a flickering white light sprang to life in my palm. It cast off a brighter, warmer glow than the phone had, completely illuminating the area around us.

Ella released me and jumped back with a yelp. "How are you doing that?"

"It won't hurt you," I said anxiously. "I know this is strange, but you have to stay calm, okay? I'll explain everything, I promise."

Ella backed away from me, her eyes locked on the flame in my palm.

"Ella... I'm a witch," I told her. My voice trembled as I spoke. "We were transported here by a spell that was cast over the old Sinclair site. I don't know exactly what happened, but I'm sure that everything happening here has to do with magic. The thefts at the museum, the cold snap we're dealing with... everything."

"I must be having a fever dream," Ella murmured, pressing her hand to her forehead.

I waited for her to decide what she was going to do. Thoughts of revealing myself had flitted through my head before, but I'd never told anyone. Even as a child, the knowledge that I could never reveal my secret had been too powerful for me to ignore.

Right now, I felt like I might end up at the bottom of a lake with cement shoes. Not that I believed Ella would hurt me, but I'd broken the cardinal rule… What would the consequences be?

Ella shook her head hard. "Let's look around."

Well, at least she wasn't freaking out. I inspected our surroundings. Beneath our feet was a map of the town. As I knelt to get a closer look at it, light flooded the cave. I flinched as my eyes strained.

Ella stood next to a camping lantern that cast off enough light to see the entire room clearly. I extinguished my flame, staring at it with low spirits. So if I had only kept my cellphone on long enough to take a better look around, I wouldn't have had to reveal myself to Ella.

"It looks like someone lives out here," Ella said. A camping cot was set up along one wall, with a propane stove, a package of bottled water, and other gear next to it.

"They carved a map of the town into the floor," I said, standing. As I turned in a slow circle, I nodded. "This is where our thief has been holding out. Look. There's the handkerchief, teacup, kettle, iron, and plow from the museum."

"Why would they take all this just to hide it in a cave?" Ella wondered aloud.

I stepped over to the kettle and frowned. "Ella, look at this. This kettle belonged to Herbet Sinclair, right? And it's put right where his original house was built."

Ella frowned and hurried over to the plow. "This is where the Mercer family built their first house."

She stooped and picked up a piece of paper.

"He must have found where the original structures were and brought these items here to perform a spell," I murmured.

"Harper?"

I turned back to Ella.

"This is Max's writing. We were researching…" She held the paper out to me, then dug her hands into her honey-brown hair. "It only says 'center of the ley lines' and then 'net.' What does this mean?"

"Ley lines are alignments of magical currents within the earth's surface," I told her, bending to the map again. "We know the Whit-mans had magic, and if Max Harrington is a witch, then it's likely he inherited his magic books from his ancestry."

Ella's eyes were round as saucers as she stared at me.

I laid my hand on the map. "Maybe the other families were magical as well. If they were…"

I nudged a little magic into it. All the lines lit up. The roads glowed pale blue, the buildings green. And over it all, connecting the five spots where the original structures were built, were the golden ley lines. It formed a net over the town.

"Just what I thought. These are where the ley lines run," I told her, straightening. "By building on these spots, the founding families created a net of magic over the town. They would have been able to use it for protection or to make the weather better for crops. Liam said that Moonhaven is much more mild than the surrounding area."

"Then… then something went wrong?" Ella asked incredulously. "To make it turn cold like this?"

"They fought over land and power. So, they lost the connection to each other… and during the Winter Festival, Percival Whitman did more than just attack David," I explained. "He called on ancestral magic to do so. The net must have caught it and amplified it, even after he was jailed."

"How do we break it, then?"

I winced as I turned to her. "This part is where things get weird."

Ella frowned at me. "I'm not sure how it can get weirder."

"The spell has focused on you. You're not sick because the town is cold… the town is cold because you're sick. The net didn't dispel the spell over the town. It focused it on you, the living descendant of the five people who put it into place four hundred years ago."

"I…" She looked horrified, and I couldn't blame her. "But… all these things…"

"I don't know why he did this. What he hopes to get from it," I said, shaking my head. "Liam already suspected Max Harrington was behind the museum thefts. And with this," I lifted the paper with his writing on it. "It's proof. He used magic to steal all these things."

Ella stiffened. To my surprise, her eyes flashed with anger. "Max is my friend. He would never hurt me. I'd sooner believe you were doing this."

I stepped back, hurt.

"And I don't believe you're behind it, either," Ella said, softening again. "But I can't believe Max has anything to do with it. I can't believe any of it... If my ancestors had magic, why don't I?"

"Magic isn't inherited, it's taught. I could teach you how to use magic," I said. "But it's passed on from parent to child. Only, some people decide not to teach their children. Ever since the witch trials, we've been more and more secretive. A lot of knowledge was lost. I don't even know if Percival was taught magic as a child or found the rituals later in life."

Ella rubbed her eyes, then sighed. "This really is all too much for me to understand. But are you sure it's because I'm a descendant of all of them?"

"I can't see another reason."

"My coffee shop." She pointed at the map. "It's where the first Town Hall was built."

I followed where she was pointing. All the ley lines of the area converged into a central spot... right on her coffee shop. I stared hard, watching the pulsing golden lights. If that was where Town Hall had once been... the bell was taken for a reason. These things were taken for a reason.

Ella was certain Max wouldn't hurt her.

"Oh," I whispered.

"What is it?"

"I think I know what's really happening... but we have to get out of here," I said, rushing to grab Ella's hand. "We have little time."

# CHAPTER 5
## THE EQUINOX RITUAL

Ella's teeth were chattering as Liam put a blanket around her shoulders. He reached into the cruiser for a second one for me, but I shook my head.

"Ella needs it more than I do."

She was so exhausted that she didn't protest. Liam helped her into the backseat, where she buckled herself in and promptly sagged against the backrest. I threw my arms around Liam, burying my face into his puffy jacket.

"I was worried I'd given you the wrong directions," I told him.

Liam hugged me back tightly. "What happened?"

I sighed. When Ella and I had navigated out of the cave, I'd only had enough battery life on my phone to give Liam a quick call. I wasn't sure how I was going to explain the whole magical transportation part of things.

"We found a cave with the things that were stolen from the museum," I said as we got into the car. The heat was blowing, warming up my frigid fingers. Liam drove as I continued, "And Ella found a piece of paper with Max Harrington's handwriting on it."

"It wasn't him," Ella insisted sleepily from the back.

Snow drifted down from the sky. I peered at the dark gray clouds in worry. Everything seemed so still and silent... and Ella falling asleep like this could be just from exhaustion, or it could be the spell kicking up another notch.

"How did you find the cave?" Liam asked.

"Tracks in the snow."

Liam glanced at me, his expression frustrated, but didn't search me long. He turned back to the road.

I cleared my throat. "But Max's handwriting proves it was him, right?"

"It's evidence, not proof of anything," Liam reminded me. "And it doesn't say why he's doing any of this."

"Max isn't behind it," Ella said again. "He's my friend. He would never."

I chewed my lip. That was precisely why he was doing it. Hadn't Abigail told me to find the heart of the thief? That was exactly it. Max Harrington loved Ella. It didn't matter if it was a romantic or platonic love—what mattered was that he loved her and wanted to save her.

The only thing was, I couldn't tell Liam any of this. He'd never understand, even if he believed it.

"We need to get to the coffee shop right away," I said.

Liam glanced in the rearview mirror at Ella and nodded. I leaned back, twisting the seat belt in my hands. Ironic that Ella named the shop 'Ella's Wheel' when it was the hub of the ley lines. I wondered how she had got it. Was it inherited or had she bought the place? Did she rent it? How deeply her connection ran would impact how to break the spell laying over her.

"Are we almost there?" Ella asked in a thin voice. She slumped over with a sudden sigh, and my heart jumped.

"Ella?" I called.

Nothing.

Liam's hands tightened on the steering wheel. "She needs a hospital."

"No."

"What are you—she needs a doctor!" Liam shouted incredulously.

I twisted in my seat, sticking my fingers through the cage-like barrier that separated the back from the front. Ella's breathing was deep. Her cheeks were pink, her body relaxed. She looked like she was sleeping soundly.

"We need to get to the coffee shop," I repeated.

"Harper—"

I twisted around again. "Liam, trust me. This is like the Winter Festival all over again. Doctors won't be able to help her. We need to get to the coffee shop. It's where Max is."

Liam's jaw clenched. A muscle ticked in his forehead, but he turned off the main road, twisting through the streets until we got to the coffee shop. Once we were there, I jumped from the cruiser and rushed inside. Max Harrington laid on the floor, his face white. Beneath him was a crudely drawn picture of the map, much like what we'd seen in the cave. Only, instead of the artifacts marking the spots where the original buildings were, there were photocopied portraits of the five founders.

I dropped to my knees next to him, checking his pulse. It was erratic and weak, and his skin was frosty. Beneath his fingers was a picture of him and Ella as children.

"What's going on?" Liam demanded from the doorway.

I turned and gasped. Ella was standing beside him. Soft, wavering, looking confused… Liam looked to where she was but didn't see her. Of course he didn't. It was only her spirit here, the same sort of flickering way I'd seen David Blackwood's spirit during the Winter Festival.

"Ella?"

I whirled to find Max's spirit standing nearby. He flickered, unstable, the same way Ella was. My heart jack rabbited in my chest. Their spirits had distended from their bodies. It wouldn't take much for the tethers that kept them alive to snap and kill them both.

"Ella, I'm sorry," Max said, sounding like he was coming from a far distance. "I thought I could transfer the curse to me. I thought I could save you."

"Harper!" Liam strode forward and grabbed my shoulders, breaking me from my growing horror. "What is going on?"

"Bring Ella in here," I blurted.

He opened his mouth to argue.

"Please," I begged. "Bring her in here. I don't have much time. Trust me."

Liam screwed his eyes shut. He hesitated, and I held my breath. I couldn't do this without him. Forget about keeping magic a secret. This was about the lives of two people, not to mention the fate of the whole town.

"I need you," I whispered.

His eyes opened, full of determination. "You'll owe me an explanation."

He was off before I could answer. I arranged the photocopied portraits on the floor, whispering a spell to adhere each one to the map. A bell tolled in the distance as Liam brought Ella in. I had him lay her down next to Max and pressed their hands together while laying the picture of the two of them right over where the coffee shop was on the map.

"Give me your hand and close your eyes," I told Liam.

His fingers were calloused and his grip firm, but the warmth of his hand gave me hope. I held out my other hand, summoning my revealing winds. They whipped around us. Liam gasped, his eyes still tightly shut. The bell rang harder, louder; the sound echoing through the coffee shop.

So this is where the bell went when Max stole it. He returned it to the spot where it had hung in Town Hall four hundred years ago.

A shimmering tangle of red lines appeared over the map, wrapping Max and Ella up in a twisting net that grew tighter even as I watched. They weren't crisscrossed in the same pattern as the ley lines on the map, though—this net was the spell. It shivered as it tightened, edges curling up and then laying flat again like an octopus.

I released Liam's hand and raced forward as a new rope crawled over their bodies. It twisted in my hand like a snake when I grabbed it. I wrestled it back to the spot where it started from, grunting with the effort. When I touched the raw ends together, it disappeared.

"It's nearing the twelfth stroke," Liam called as the bell tolled again.

My heart stopped. Twelfth stroke. It wasn't anywhere near twelve, be that midnight or midday, but the bell didn't care. We were close enough to the equinox. Max's interference must have sped up the process of it all.

"Help me," I said.

Liam opened his eyes and gasped. "What—"

"We need to get them free of the light," I panted, struggling with the next rope. "Hurry! Please!"

Liam sprang into action. He rushed forward, grabbing onto the rope I struggled with. He planted his feet as he helped me pull it back, yanking relentlessly as I detangled it from the others. Slowly, one by one, we released the net. The ropes still in place shriveled, tightening on Ella and Max.

The last one was across their necks. It wrapped around, wriggling like a snake wanting to strangle them. I lunged and grabbed one side while Liam caught the other side.

The bell tolled twelve and an awful crashing filled the coffee shop. The ceiling burst open, sending wooden shrapnel everywhere. The heavy thing fell directly toward Liam. I screamed but had no time to summon my winds. It struck him, sending him flying, before it crushed the brew bar and rolled toward Max and Ella.

I leaped forward, the rope still gripped in one hand as I braced myself. It knocked into me, sending me stumbling backward, but the bell rolled to a stop before it crushed them. The rope in my hand disappeared and everything fell silent.

Ella groaned. She and Max were both stirring, looking drained and confused.

I rushed to Liam. He lay motionless. Blood soaked through his hair and I ripped off my sweater to press to the gash on his scalp. His skin was pale, but he was breathing visibly.

"Max, call the ambulance," I yelled over my shoulder.

He groaned in response. "What happened?"

"Call the ambulance," I repeated.

"Give me your phone," Ella said. She called the ambulance while I held onto Liam, shaking with fear. How serious was this? What if the bell had done permanent damage?

Max crawled over beside me. He pushed a book toward me; it was bound in green leather with the image of standing stones on the front. His gaze was still confused, but he silently put his hands over mine, pressing down on Liam's injury to prevent more bleeding.

"I don't know what to do," he rasped. "Ella has to perform the ritual."

# CHAPTER 6
# REBIRTH OF TRUTH

My finger pressed to the page, underlining the words describing the ritual I was meant to do. Ella wrapped her arms around herself, shivering despite the warmth of the room. I hurried back to her side and pulled her into the center of the map. The portraits were still in place, so I backed off the map.

"Hold your hand out and touch the bell," I instructed.

She did so; her face rapidly turning more ashen. Outside, the wind howled, driving snow into the window with such force it was almost hail. The sky turned dark.

Holding both my hands upward, I summoned my winds. They whipped through the room, picking up the portraits.

"The curses of those who have gone before are broken," I called. "Release her by the blood of her ancestors."

Outside, the wind died suddenly and the hail-like snow turned to a soft, pattering rain. The sink behind the brew bar streamed with water and the giant hole in the ceiling disappeared, along with the bell. The portraits disappeared in green flames and all went still.

Ella pulled in a deep breath, the color returning to her face. She stood straight, no longer trembling. "Is it done?"

I nodded, my shoulders slumping. "It's done. You're free."

The sound of sirens took our attention. Ella hurried to the door to talk to the paramedics while I returned to Liam, kneeling next to him. He was even paler than before, but his breathing was still even. I checked his pulse and was relieved when I found it strong.

The paramedics took Liam away, leaving Ella, Max, and me to clean up the rest of the coffee shop. While the hole in the ceiling had fixed itself, the lights were still scattered all over the floor, along with giant chunks of plaster.

"Where do you think the bell went?" Max asked, subdued.

"That depends. Are you the one that took it?"

Max shook his head. "I knew it would come back here with the spell. I thought it wouldn't come until tomorrow. I thought I had a day left to fix it."

He bowed his head, his shoulders slumping.

Ella stepped up beside him and touched his elbow. "So you were doing all of this to save me? When I didn't even know something was wrong?"

"Yeah. After what happened at the Winter Festival, I thought that the things my grandfather used to tell me were real after all. I've been reading everything I could find, but..." He lifted his head and stared at me, his brow furrowed. "But I don't know as much as you do."

"You're not a witch. Not yet, at least," I said awkwardly. "You tried to take the spell off Ella and put it on yourself."

Ella gasped.

"That's where you went wrong. You don't have the ancestry she does, so it only made the curses laid on the Harrington line stronger," I explained.

Max let out a shaky breath.

"It worked out this time, but don't use magic without proper guidance again," I warned him. "Not only is it dangerous to you, but it's dangerous to all of us. You two might not be witches, might not have the training, but the witch hunters won't care."

Ella's eyes turned round. "Witch hunters?"

I shivered. "I'll tell you about them later. Just know that they exist. And for that reason, you must tell no one what happened here. Nobody can know."

Both of them nodded seriously. I hoped that they'd take my warnings to heart. My hands shook with anxiety as I grabbed a broom. In a single day, I'd revealed my magic to not one, but three people. What would the repercussions be?

"You should get to the hospital to check on Liam," Ella said.

I flinched. My stomach twisted as my blood ran even colder. I was trying to distract myself from the worry, hoping that if I kept busy, I might skip the awful waiting. What would I do if he didn't recover? There was so much blood.

"Harper." Ella put her arms around me as I crumpled inward. "You should be there when he wakes up."

My chest hurt, but I nodded. "I can't drive myself."

"We'll drive you," Max said. "Then maybe swing by the museum and see if the bell came back."

Ella smiled at him. "Maybe even go out to that cave and take back everything you stole?"

He blushed and ducked his head.

Outside, nearly all the snow had been melted by the rain already. The yards, once hidden, were vibrant green. There were even a few flowers already growing here and there. I sighed; this meant the spell was truly broken.

Ella would be okay.

Max sighed as well as we got into the car. "I want to help Moonhaven. There are so many deep hurts caused by the disputes of the past. I wish there was more I could do."

"We'll keep working on that," I told him. "Moonhaven is a powerfully magical place. But you have to be ready to face punishment for your thefts, Max. I don't think Liam will turn a blind eye to this."

My stomach cramped again. Liam would get better. He had to. Which meant, of course, he was going to throw the book at Max… and demand answers from me. I wasn't sure what I'd tell him yet, but I'd think of something. The truth was always a good idea. There certainly were no lies that would trick him after what he saw.

As we drove, Ella leaned forward and wrapped her arms around me. "I think I understand."

"Understand?" I repeated, confused.

"Why you didn't tell me? I mean, obviously, there's stuff to it I don't know. Witch hunters and all that... but even without that, I understand why you wouldn't tell me you're a witch. It must be lonely, having a secret like that... something that, if the truth got out, you don't know if you'd be safe or not."

Tears flooded my eyes. That was exactly what I felt.

"I will always be your friend, Harper," Ella promised me. "Always."

Sniffing, I nodded.

They dropped me off at the front of the hospital and made me promise to tell them as soon as I had any updates. I headed into the hospital, my steps heavy. To my surprise, I found Abigail was already in Liam's room when I was brought there. Her cloud of gray hair was loose around her shoulders and her eyes were closed.

I never would have figured out what was going on with Max if it weren't for her cryptic advice two days ago. It seemed so much longer than that.

She opened her eyes and smiled at me as I sank into the chair next to her. "I was wondering when you'd get here."

"How is he?" I asked, looking anxiously at him.

His breathing was even, and his color better than it had been in the coffee shop. His head was bandaged, and an IV dripped into his arm. I laced my fingers together as I searched the room for any sign of how bad it was.

"He has a concussion and needed stitches to close up that gash in his scalp, but he'll be fine," Abigail said.

I slumped back in my chair, covering my face. Relief swept through me as I struggled to breathe evenly. Part of me wanted to cry in sheer relief.

Abigail rubbed my back. "I just sent Ella a text before you came in. Do you know what happened?"

I shook my head, unable to talk about it. We'd told the paramedics that the light fixture had broken free and struck Liam's head. I hoped it was a good enough explanation to stick.

"How do you know so much about what goes on in this town?" I blurted, looking up at Abigail. She always seemed to know what was going on… was it just a coincidence?

Abigail shrugged. "Moonhaven holds many secrets. When you're old enough, you see them much clearer."

Before I could ask her what she meant, Liam groaned.

I leaned forward, grasping his hand. "Liam?"

His eyes opened and squished back shut. "Ugh. I haven't had a hangover like this since… ever."

I laughed shakily.

Abigail patted my shoulder. "I'll go get the doctors."

"Doctors?" Liam opened his eyes again. He squinted blearily at me.

I rubbed my thumb over his knuckles. "You don't think I'd leave you after hitting your head like that, do you?"

Liam reached up to touch his head, a bewildered expression on his face. "Did I slip on the ice or something?"

"No, you—" I cut myself off. Slip on the ice? My heart pounded. "What do you remember last?"

"We were walking, and you were talking about the spring equinox."

I straightened. "Liam… that was two days ago. You hit your head in the coffee shop. Don't you remember?"

His gaze met mine. Confusion swam in his eyes. I held my breath as I stared back. So this meant he had no memory of the last two days? No memory of the ritual we'd performed to save Ella and Max? I should be relieved, but I… I couldn't tell if I was. Or if some part of me was upset that he didn't know my secret.

It was good news for Max, though. So long as he and Ella returned the items he stole without being caught, it meant Liam wouldn't keep looking for the thief.

"Harper?" Liam asked me. He sounded… vulnerable.

I squeezed his hand. "It's all going to be fine. You're okay, and I'll tell you what happened these last two days."

Not all of it, though. Never all of it. I forced a smile at him and kissed his cheek, surprising myself.

"I'm staying with you," I told him. "I'm going to take care of you."

Liam smiled back. The tension melted from his body, and he closed his eyes again. "Thank you."

Butterflies swarmed my stomach. But along with them were the seeds of guilt for the lies I was already preparing for him. I had no choice. The number one rule of being a witch was to tell nobody.

But Liam was alive. He wasn't badly injured. I squeezed his hand again. Everything was going to be just fine.

The End.

Did you enjoy *Spring Break*?

Please consider rating it on Goodreads, Bookbub or your favorite retailers.

Reviews help me reach new readers.

**Read all the books in the Cozy Mystery Samplers.**

Read all the stories

*Jane and Kennedy Daniels Mysteries*

*Pine Grove Mysteries*

*Wilma Wade Holiday Mysteries*

*Mike and Maddie Mysteries*

*Mystic Moonhaven Mysteries*

*Annie Archer Paranormal Mysteries*

**Join my Newsletter for updates and giveaways!**

**www.daisylandishromance.com**